BOOKS BY DAVID WALLIAMS:

The Boy in the Dress
Mr Stink
Billionaire Boy
Gangsta Granny
Ratburger
Demon Dentist
Awful Auntie
Grandpa's Great Escape
The Midnight Gang
Bad Dad
The Ice Monster
The Beast of Buckingham Palace
Code Name Bananas
Gangsta Granny Strikes Again!

Fing
Slime
Megamonster

The World's Worst Children
The World's Worst Children 2
The World's Worst Children 3
The World's Worst Teachers
The World's Worst Parents

ALSO AVAILABLE IN PICTURE BOOK:

The Slightly Annoying Elephant
The First Hippo on the Moon
The Bear Who Went Boo!
The Queen's Orang-utan
There's a Snake in My School!
Boogie Bear
Geronimo
The Creature Choir
Little Monsters
Marmalade

David Walliams

THE WORLD'S WORST

PETS

Illustrated in fabulous colour by

Adam Stower

HarperCollins Children's Books

DAVID WALLIAMS

For Lyla, Raffy
and Cleo,
with love – David x

ADAM STOWER

For Emily and Isabel,
with love – A.S.

First published in the United Kingdom by HarperCollins *Children's Books* in 2022
HarperCollins *Children's Books* is a division of HarperCollins*Publishers* Ltd,
1 London Bridge Street, London SE1 9GF
www.harpercollins.co.uk
HarperCollins*Publishers*, 1st Floor, Watermarque Building, Ringsend Road,
Dublin 4, Ireland

2

Text copyright © David Walliams 2022
Illustrations copyright © Adam Stower 2022
Cover lettering of author's name copyright © Quentin Blake 2010
All rights reserved.
HB ISBN 978-0-00-830580-2
TPB ISBN 978-0-00-849977-8

THANK-YOUS

I would like to thank this gang of animal fans who helped me with the book...

Adam Stower, *my illustrator*, would love to be a bear, as he likes the sound of bumbling about in the woods, eating honey and snoozing all through the winter.

Executive Publisher **Ann-Janine Murtagh** would most like to be a tiger – a wild one – as it is rare, beautiful, agile and intelligent. Although obviously not the most suitable choice for a pet!

HarperCollins CEO, **Charlie Redmayne,** would be a cat, because they sleep all day and the world rotates around them.

My literary agent, **Paul Stevens**, would like to be a polar bear, as he has always been fascinated by them because of their power and beauty.

My editor, **Nick Lake,** would be an octopus so he could read, work and play with his kids all at once. In reality he would probably just eat eight chocolate bars in one go.

Art Editor **Kate Burns** would love to be her own Speagle dog. All his days are spent mooching, loafing and tolerating hugs, which seems like the best kind of life to have. Goals.

Publishing Manager **Samantha Stewart** would most like to be a harpy eagle, because of flying, obviously, but also because they are so ferocious no editor would dare argue with them about capital letters or full stops...

Creative Director **Val Brathwaite** would like to be a bunny as they are highly intelligent, very sociable and affectionate. Her first pet was a bunny who lived to the ripe old age of 11 years.

Designer **Kate Clarke** has always longed to be a dolphin. Smart, graceful, curious – they are everything she aims to be.

Designer **Elorine Grant** wants to be a cheetah, so she can hunt down her enemies.

Designer **Matthew Kelly** wants to be a kiwi so he can stay out all night!

Designer **Sally Griffin** sometimes dreams of being a dog so she could have a proper natter with her pet Schnauzer. Woof woof woof!

My audio editor, **Tanya Hougham,** would be a red-capped manakin – she likes to dress in bright colours and loves to dance... even when asked not to.

Head of Marketing, **Alex Cowan,** would choose to be a flamingo, because they're pink and fabulous, with long legs, like him. (The long legs bit. Not the pink bit.)

My PR Director, **Geraldine Stroud,** would be a lioness, as she is keen to be queen of the jungle!

David Walliams

INTRODUCTION

Most pets are cute and cuddly. They give you *love* and make you **happy.** You hold them. You stroke them. You might even wipe your nose on them. It is best not to, as they really don't like it.

However, there are pets that cause devastation, distress and despair.

These are the pets I will be telling you about in this book. They are so much more **fun** than the nice ones.

We have met the world's worst children, the world's worst teachers and even the world's worst parents.

Now you must prepare yourself for the absolute worst of the worst...

THE WORLD'S WORST PETS!

David Walliams

CONTENTS

Furp
the FISH

Many years ago, decades before you were born, there stood a long-forgotten seaside town, with a rickety old pier that stretched out into the sea. At the end of the pier was a fair run by grumpy old folk with weather-beaten faces, and battered hats and coats.

It wasn't a fair fair. Locals called it THE **UNFAIR FAIR,** because at this fair nobody ever won anything.

It was impossible to:

knock the **coconut** off its post,

or boot the **football** through the hole,

or hook the **duck** and win a goldfish.

That is until the day our story begins.

"I GOT ONE!" exclaimed a boy, bouncing up and down in his battered shoes. His name was Leo, and he had never been so excited in all his little life.

Behind the stall, the lizard of a man spat out his cigarette.

"You what?"

"I HOOKED A DUCK!"

Indeed, Leo had. On the end of the fishing rod was a battered toy duck.

"You cheated!" snarled the stallholder.

"No! I didn't!" protested Leo. "I was just lucky, and I am never, ever lucky!"

Little did he know how **unlucky** he was about to become.

The man grumbled and grunted. It was clear no one had ever managed to hook one of his ducks before.

"Sorry, sir, but do I win a prize?" asked Leo with a hopeful smile.

It was met with a **sinister** grin. The old man sniggered to himself as he reached under the counter. With some difficulty, he lifted up a goldfish.

Now, I know what you are thinking: how could a goldfish be one of the world's worst pets? Well, this was no ordinary goldfish. This was the biggest goldfish that ever lived. The goldfish was so large that it seemed **bigger** than the bowl in which it was swimming.

A goldfish is normally **this** big.

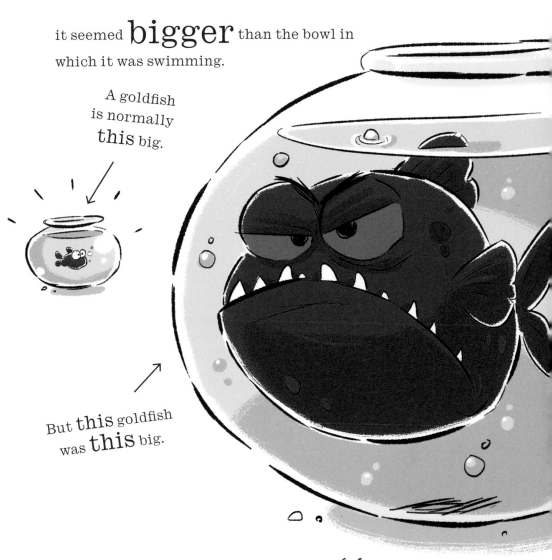

But **this** goldfish was **this** big.

Leo peered through the glass and *smiled* at his new pet. The creature had **bulging** eyes and big **SHARP** teeth.

It opened its angry mouth wide and began chomping at the glass.

CHOMP! CHOMP! CHOMP!

It was as if it wanted to eat the boy!

"Make sure you feed it!" chuckled the man.

"It looks like I will have to!"

"This fish gets very, very hungry."

"What does it eat?"

"Everything! Ha! Ha!"

Leo wasn't sure why this was funny. "Does it have a name?"

"Furp!"

"Furp? That's a weird name for a fish. Weird name for anything. Why is it called Furp?"

"Oh-ho! You'll see! And hear! And... smell!" replied the man with another snigger.

"Thank you, I think," replied Leo as he stumbled off, carrying the bowl. The water sploshed around, with Furp leaping out of the bowl as it chomped at the air.

CHOMP! CHOMP! CHOMP!

*

"Leo! No! What did you bring that great **ugly** thing back for?" thundered his Aunt Beatie. Beatie ran a guesthouse at the seaside – **Beatie's Bed & Breakfast***.

Not that anyone stayed at **Beatie's Bed & Breakfast.** Beatie was a **dragon** of a lady, who breathed **fire** on her guests.

Now, the only guest was her unlucky nephew. Oh, and Beatie's fearsome cat, **Curdle.** More of her **later!**

Poor Leo endured the grave misfortune of being packed off to stay with his appalling aunt **every** single summer.

* Breakfast not included.

"Sorry, Aunt Beatie! I won it at the **FAIR!**" replied Leo, proudly holding up the bowl. "I guess I was lucky."

The lady pressed her hooter up against the glass, smearing it with grease. Furp chomped at it from the other side.

CHOMP! CHOMP! CHOMP!

"Unlucky, by the look of it!" she replied, banging the glass. "What on earth is it?"

"It's a goldfish!"

"This great brute?"

"Furp is special."

"FURP?" she thundered.

"Yes. Its name is Furp."

"Stupid name for a fish! I'll flush it down the bog!" she said, snatching it away.

"Nooo!" cried Leo.

Furp must have understood, because it leaped out of its bowl and went to CHOMP Beatie's nose.

CHOMP!

It couldn't reach, so plunged back into the bowl.

SPLOSH!

"Well, what if Curdle gobbles down your fish? Sort of unlucky thing that happens to you! I don't want you bawling your eyes out! Spraying your tears all over my nice carpet! CURDLE!"

Aunt Beatie's fearsome cat Curdle snaked out of the shadows. It leaped up on to its mistress's shoulder.

"My little furry angel!" she said as she tickled the sinister creature under its chin. "Look what we have here, Curdle! Your din-dins!"

The cat's eyes widened as it stared through the glass, bared its fangs and licked its lips.

"**HISS!**"

"Furp can stay down in the cellar with me!" said Leo. "And I will keep the door shut to keep Curdle out!"

The cat reached out its paw, and *swiped* at the bowl, its razor-sharp claws clinking against the glass.

TINK! TONK! TUNK!

From the other side of the glass, Furp opened its mouth wide, baring its **FANGS.**

 **CHOMP!**

In fear, the cat leaped up on to Aunt Beatie's head.

"MIAOW!"

Curdle's paws scrabbled for footing on the lady's eyebrows.

"**HISS!**" hissed the cat.

"GET THAT EVIL BEAST OUT OF MY SIGHT!" bawled Aunt Beatie. "How dare it terrify my darling little Curdle!" she added, thrusting the bowl back to the boy.

"Sorry, Aunt Beatie!"

Leo ran down the stairs to the tiny basement in the depths of the guesthouse. It was by far the worst room in the place, such was his luck. Immediately, he shut the door so the cat couldn't get in.

He set the bowl down on a table. Then he dipped his finger into the water to give his pet a stroke.

"Here, Furpy! Here, fishy!"

Instantly the creature bit into it.

CHOMP!

"YEOW!" screamed Leo.

Furp wouldn't let go.

Instead, the creature dug its sharp teeth deeper and

deeper into Leo's finger. The man on the end of the pier was right. This was one hungry fish!

"YEOW!" screamed Leo again. Not that it did much good.

He raced around the cellar, flapping his hand wildly, trying to shake the thing off.

However, the more Leo shook, the **deeper** Furp bit.

"YEOW!"

Leo bounced up and down on the bed.

BOING! BOING! BOING!

Still the fish **wouldn't** let go.

Next, he stood upside down in the

wardrobe.

CLONK!

Still the fish **wouldn't** let go.

Finally, he performed a cartwheel

across the floor.

THOMP! THOMP! THOMP!

STILL THE FISH WOULDN'T LET GO!

Leo needed to find some food, and fast. With the

whopper still attached to his finger, he rushed

out of the cellar. In a panic, he left the door wide open!

OOPS!

The boy raced up the steep flight of stairs to the kitchen.

What do goldfish eat? he thought as he swung open the fridge door.

Plankton? There weren't any.

Tadpoles? No. **Not one!**

Algae? There was something green and slimy growing up the back of the fridge, but Leo was pretty sure that was just **mould.**

But before Leo's eyes had scoured all the shelves the fish flapped **off** his finger and plunged itself into a bowl of **trifle!**

SPLOOSH!

CHOMP!

Trifle was Aunt Beatie's favourite. She would eat a **whole** one for breakfast!

The fish flapped around in the glass bowl, now at least **twice** the size it had been before. Its tummy was as big and round as a football, hardly surprising as it had a whole trifle inside it. Then it let out the most tremendous noise. It sounded like someone blowing into

a tuba – someone who had absolutely
no ability to play it.

BLURGH!

At once, Leo realised he was witnessing the rarest
of all phenomena.

The "furp".

The furp is when someone, or something, farts and
burps at precisely the same time.

Leo thought the furp was the stuff of legend. An
ancient myth. A playground fable. But no. Furps were
real.

No wonder Furp was called "Furp". Furp was a furper!

If the sound was unpleasant, the smell was
appalling!

Leo began to choke, and his eyes streamed.

The wallpaper in Beatie's Bed & Breakfast even
began peeling off the walls!

RIP!

Leo thought he was going to pass out!

He lifted the bowl and raced back down to

the cellar. It was only then that he realised he'd left the door wide open!

Oh no!

Leo scoured the room for Aunt Beatie's terrifying pet, but couldn't see it anywhere.

"Curdle? Curdle?" he called out, but there was no reply. Not even the faintest miaow.

So, Leo slammed the door…

BANG!

…and poured his fish back into its fishbowl. As it fell through the air, Furp furped again.

BLURGH!

The fish furped with such **furptastic force** that it shot into its bowl like a rocket.

SPLOOSH!

Leo looked down at his **troublesome** pet. It was gazing up at him with its mouth wide open, ready to pounce.

CHOMP! CHOMP! CHOMP! went the fish, snapping its jaws together.

The chomping could mean only one thing. Furp needed feeding **again!**

"FURP! You just ate a **whole trifle!**" exclaimed Leo.

CHOMP! came the reply.

"But I haven't got any more food!"

Furp looked over to the biscuit tin on the shelf. During the summer, Leo lived off the tins of biscuits his parents sent him.

"Sorry, Furp!" said Leo. "I scoffed all the biscuits last week!"

CHOMP! it chomped again.

"But hold on a moment!" He raced over to his bed. "I'm a messy eater! You might just be in luck!"

Leo whipped off the bedcover to reveal a layer of biscuit crumbs on the mattress. There were so many crumbs that he could make a whole new biscuit! He wet his finger before picking up **crumb** after **crumb.**

Next, he squeezed the crumbs all together in his sweaty palm, calling out, "Your after-dinner snack is coming right up, Furp!"

However, behind him he heard a deafening **CHOMP!**

Leo spun round. He rushed over to the bowl, expecting to see that the fish had been gobbled up by the cat. But when Leo peered down into the water he realised the opposite had happened! Furp coughed up a fur ball!

A ginger fur ball!

"HURGH!"

Then the fish did something Leo had never seen a fish do before. It smiled. Not a nice smile, either. A sinister smile!

Leo gulped in HORROR! This was no ordinary goldfish! This was a **MONSTER!**

What on earth would he tell his aunt Beatie? First her trifle had been eaten, now her cat!

With the animal in its tummy, the fish was now far too big for the bowl. Only its head was stuck in it, and its bottom furped right in Leo's direction.

BLURGH!

In desperation, he raced up five flights of stairs, carrying the bowl. Up there was the guesthouse's one and only bath. Leo raced in and spun the taps to fill the bath as quickly as he could.

WHOOOSH!

As soon as there was enough water, he emptied his troublesome pet into its new home.

SPLOOSH!

The giant goldfish seemed happy for a moment as it splashed around. The beast leaped in and out of the water as if putting on a show.

SPLOSH!
SPLOSH!
SPLOSH!

But then...

CHOMP!

...it scoffed Beatie's bar of soap. Then the fish began frothing at the mouth!

BLUB! BLUB! BLUB!

"FURP! FURP! FURP!" went Furp as bubbles sprayed from both ends of the beast.

Soon the entire bathroom was a **bubble riot.**

"Oh no!" cried Leo.

"WHAT'S ALL THAT NOISE?" demanded a voice from downstairs.

"Just running your bath, Aunt Beatie!" shouted Leo.

CHOMP!

"OH NO! NO! NO!" exclaimed Leo.

The monster needed feeding AGAIN!

Leo raced out of the bathroom, and back down the stairs. He desperately needed to find something else for his hungry pet to eat. However, halfway down, he bumped straight into Aunt Beatie.

BOINK!

"EURGH!" she yelled.

"Sorry, Aunt Beatie!"

Her face glowed **puce** with fury. It clashed with her matching maroon dressing gown and fluffy slippers.

"You stupid oaf! Look where you are going!" she thundered.

"Sorry!"

"And stop saying sorry!"

"Sorry! Oops! Sorry!" said Leo, getting all in a tizz.

"Have you seen Curdle recently?"

"Not that recently," replied Leo, only half fibbing.

"I can't find my darling anywhere!"

"I will keep my eyes peeled!" said the boy. "Gotta go!"

With that, he raced back down into the kitchen. But as soon as he opened the larder door in search of food, a terrible thought flashed across his mind. Aunt Beatie was about to have her bath!

"NOOOOOOOOOOOOOOOO!" cried Leo, dashing out of the kitchen and hurling himself back up the stairs. "AUNT BEATIE! STOP!"

She was standing in the bathroom doorway.

"How dare you? I always take my bath first! You can use my cold and dirty bathwater after!" she thundered, slamming the bathroom door in his face.

SHUNT!

"PLEASE! OPEN UP!" begged Leo as he pounded his fists on the door.

BANG! BANG! BANG!

"BOG OFF!"

"WHATEVER YOU DO, DON'T GET IN THE—"

But before Leo could say "bath", there was a scream.

"AAARRRGGGHHH!"

Then he heard water being hurled about.

SPLISH! SPLASH! SPLOSH!

Leo launched his body at the bathroom door, smashing it off its hinges.

BAAAM!

The door fell to the floor with a **THUD!**

Leo cried out, "AUNT BEATIE!"

But he was too late. There was no sign of her, just a pair of fluffy slippers floating in the bath.

A deep **rumbling** sound came from under the water as the goldfish's fin skimmed the surface like a shark's.

BLURGH!

"Well, I suppose it must be nice to see Curdle again at least, Aunt Beatie!" said Leo, trying to sound **upbeat.** "You did love that cat!"

Still no response.

Now Leo had the problem of what on earth to do with a goldfish the size of a double-decker bus. Because it had eaten a **whole trifle,** a **cat** and **an auntie,** his pet was now **bigger** than the bath! It would be impossible to lift it.

Fortunately, Leo had a bright idea. — PING! —

...and began swimming underwater down to the front door. He glanced behind to see his **giant** pet snapping at his heels.

CHOMP! CHOMP! CHOMP!

If he could just avoid being eaten, this could work a treat!

Leo pulled the front door open.

The wall of water surged out!

SPLOOOOOSH!

The fish could swim away into the sea.

So the boy ran around the guesthouse, putting the plug in every sink, and turning on every tap.

WHOOSH! WHOOSH! WHOOSH! WHOOSH!

Beatie's Bed & Breakfast began filling up with water.

SPLISH! SPLASH! SPLOSH!

The water rose and rose and rose. Soon the guesthouse resembled a sunken ship. The water level reached the bath, so Furp could easily swim out.

Leo took this as his cue. He dived in…

SPLOOSH!

The water sloshed down the road like a tidal wave!

WHOOOOOOSH!

It swept Leo and Furp along the seafront. All along the way, the giant goldfish opened its jaws wide and gobbled things whole.

CHOMP! CHOMP! CHOMP!

A postbox! BLURGH!

A police car! BLURGH!

Even an ice-cream van! BLURGH!

Furp furped so loudly the entire seaside town shook.

BLLLUUUUURRRGGGHHH!

WOBBLE!

The wave swept Furp (now bigger than an airship)

along the seafront towards the pier.

SWOOSH!

Furp gobbled up the candyfloss machine and all the

candyfloss in it.

CHOMP!

"FURP!"

Next Furp gobbled all the gallopers on the carousel.

CHOMP! CHOMP! CHOMP!

BLURGH! BLURGH! BLURGH!

Then the beast ate the entire big wheel.

CHOMP! *BLURGH!*

Now Furp was the size of a whale! As the water washed away on to the beach, the fish finally came to a grinding halt at the very end of the pier.

SWISH!

The rotten wooden boards creaked under its weight.

CREAK!

Furp was now so HUMONGOUS that it cast a long, dark shadow over the man at his hook-a-duck stall.

"Sorry!" exclaimed Leo.

"No! I am not taking that thing back!" barked the man. "I warned you it was hungry!"

But, before Leo could reply, the goldfish gobbled up the

plastic ducks...

CHOMP!

...and the entire stall...

CHOMP!

...before devouring the man!

CHOMP!

"ARGH!"

Furp let out its loudest furp yet.

 BLURGH!

This furp was so **thunderous** that the entire pier

began to shake.

RUMBLE!

The boards began buckling under the weight

of the creature.

TWANG! TWONG! TWUNG!

The pier began collapsing into the sea,

taking Furp with it!

CRASH!

SPLOOSH!

Leo scrambled for his life. The boy just managed to hold on to the top of the helter-skelter as it plunged below the waves.

WHOOSH!

The goldfish then began circling the helter-skelter as it sank further below the surface.

Leo felt that **the end** was near. He pleaded with the beast to spare his life.

"PLEASE, FURP! I WILL BUY FISH FOOD NEXT TIME! I PROMISE!"

His pet powered through the water towards him, its mouth wide open to swallow him **whole**.

Leo shut his eyes tightly, ready to be eaten.

CHOMP!

Leo didn't feel a thing. He opened his eyes to see if he was still alive!

To his shock he was.

To his even greater shock, a giant octopus had reared out of the waves. It was ten times the size of Furp! What's more, it was shoving the goldfish into its mouth with its eight arms!

CHOMP! CHOMP! CHOMP!

Then he heard a sound even stranger than a furp.

"ACHUFPT!"

It was a SNURT! A sneeze, a burp and a fart all at once – that was the sound the giant octopus was making.

"ACHUFPT!"

Now Furp was no more. It was in the belly of the giant octopus, which, having captured its prey, disappeared into the depths of the ocean.

PLUNGE!

"Well, that was a stroke of luck,"
remarked Leo.

Indeed, it was.

HAMSTERS vs GERBILS

HAMSTERS AND GERBILS can be the world's best pets. However, when you put the two **together**, they become the world's worst pets!

IT'S WAR!

Let me tell you a tale…

HAMSTERS VS GERBILS

Once upon a time, there was a sweet little girl called Betsy, who was crackers about hamsters. She had hamster cuddly toys. She had posters of hamsters up on her walls. She had hamster jigsaw puzzles. She had jumpers with hamsters on them. She even wore hamster slippers. Not made from real hamsters, though. That would be cruel. Even just in a book.

But Betsy didn't have a real hamster.

After Betsy pleading, and pleading some more, her mother took her to the local pet shop on her tenth birthday. There the girl chose the cutest, fluffiest hamster you ever did see. Its soft fur was the colour of caramel and it had the pinkest, perkiest nose.

She called it Hartley. Hartley the hamster.

With her father's help, Betsy built her pet a lovely cage. It had a nest of sawdust, a toilet roll to climb through, a big wheel to spin on, a water bowl and even a little hamster house in which to sleep. Betsy kept the cage on a side table right next to her bed. That way she could play her trumpet to Hartley as he drifted off to sleep.

HOO! HOO! HOOOOOO!

The hamster would put his paws over his ears until she stopped. Then Betsy would say, "I love you even more than ice

50

cream, my beautiful little Hartley, and I always will."

Hartley smiled from ear to ear. He was the happiest hamster in the world.

However, something was about to happen that would shatter the rodent's life. Forever.

DUM! DUM! DUM!

One morning, many months later, Betsy was passing **Chomp's Pets** on her way home from school when she spotted a dear little creature in the window. She thought it was even cuter than Hartley. It looked like a hamster, but it was smaller, had a longer tail and a pointier, *perkier* and **pinkier*** nose. The little creature's fur was the shade of butter. It sat up on its back legs, and it looked straight at Betsy with its big, round eyes.

* A real made-up word you will find in the brand-new revised and updated *Walliamsictionary,* available everywhere in bargain bins.

Betsy tried to walk past, but she just couldn't.

"Excuse me?" she said as she entered the shop.

The old pet-shop owner, Mrs Chomp, was slumped on a stool. In her arms was a humongous guinea pig, as big as a beach ball, which she stroked tenderly.

"Oh, hello again, Betsy!" replied Mrs Chomp as she threw a doggie treat in the air for the guinea pig to catch in its mouth...

...before tossing another into her own mouth.

CHOMP!

CHOMP!

"How is your little hamster getting on?"

"Very well, thank you. I just wondered about the tiny buttery fellow in the window."

"Oh yes. Beautiful little chap! New in today!"

"Is he a hamster? Because I thought he could be best friends with my Hartley."

"Oh no, no, no. That's a gerbil."

"Oh."

"Gerbils are smaller than hamsters and have longer tails."

"Yes. I see," said Betsy, looking over at the creature,

who was still staring at her. "Could this gerbil and my hamster share a cage?"

"No! Never!" Mrs Chomp declared. "Legend has it that hamsters and gerbils are sworn enemies."

"Sworn enemies?" spluttered Betsy. "That's very dramatic. Why?"

"The hamster and the gerbil both consider themselves the cutest of all the rodents."

"Maybe they are both equally beautiful!"

"Would you like to buy the gerbil?" asked Mrs Chomp.

"Not today I can't," replied Betsy. "But it is my eleventh birthday soon, so perhaps if I ask Mummy and Daddy nicely…"

"You do that. I won't let anyone else buy him. I will save the little gerbil just for you!"

"Thank you!"

"I can't feel my legs any more!" cried Mrs Chomp to

the guinea pig. "OFF! OFF! OFF!"

"GGGRRR!" growled the guinea pig. It leaped down, landing with a **THUD!**

Betsy skipped out of the shop and had one last look at her new furry friend. Pressing her face up against the glass, she mouthed, "I love you!" to the gerbil.

The little darling smiled and kissed the glass.

MWAH!

All at once, Betsy's heart danced.

Now the gerbil was all she could think of. Day and night. Night and day. Gerbil! Gerbil! Gerbil!

One by one, the hamster posters on her bedroom walls

came down and were replaced by those of gerbils.

"WHAT?" Hartley the hamster muttered to himself. "Why, oh why is she putting up posters of those filthy rodents? Gerbils are hideous little creatures, always have been, always will be!"

Soon it wasn't just posters. Betsy began wearing gerbil jumpers, pyjamas and slippers. Her entire bedroom had transformed from a shrine to hamsters into a shrine to gerbils!

When Betsy's eleventh birthday finally arrived, her mother took her back to **Chomp's Pets.** Much to Betsy's delight, Mrs Chomp had kept the gerbil especially for her.

The girl skipped back home, holding her new pet in her hands. With each skip, she kissed the gerbil on his nose.

"NOOOO!" exclaimed Hartley when Betsy pranced back into her bedroom, giggling, with the creature sitting on top of her head.

"Hartley," began the girl, reaching up to take her new pet down, "I want you to meet Gerald. Gerald the gerbil."

The rodents gave each other the *evillest* stares, but smiled for the sake of appearances.

Just then, Father walked into Betsy's bedroom. "It's finally finished!" he announced, holding the biggest, shiniest cage you ever did see.

"I love it, Daddy! Thank you!" cried Betsy.

"It must be for me!" said Hartley.

"Well, we need your new pet gerbil to live in the lap of luxury!"

"GRRR!" growled the hamster. Not only was this gerbil's cage much bigger – it was also much better.

It had...

A spaghetti junction of tubes and tunnels to climb through

A snazzy water bottle that snapped on to the bars of the cage

A silver food bowl

A ladder

A swing

A slide

A hammock

To make room for Gerald's cage, Hartley's cage was shunted right up against the wall.

SHUNT!

Now the gerbil had prime position next to Betsy's bed.

As Betsy left for school the next morning, she said, "I'm sure you two will be the best of friends!"

At first, the rival rodents pretended to be nice to each other.

"Morning!" said Gerald from his cage, trying to break the ice with his new neighbour.

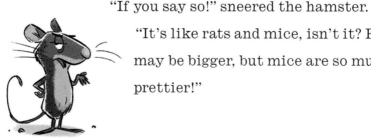

"Oh, good morning!" replied Hartley from his. "I didn't see you there!"

"I imagine I was obscured by all these super toys that my dear Betsy bought especially for me."

"No, no!" snapped Hartley. "It's just you are SO tiny! Gerbils always are!"

"Small and perfectly formed!" retorted Gerald.

"If you say so!" sneered the hamster.

"It's like rats and mice, isn't it? Rats may be bigger, but mice are so much prettier!"

"It's nothing at all like rats and mice!" declared Hartley, his tone betraying his anger.

"Oh, I think it is. Now, if you don't mind me asking—"

"Well, actually, I do! I do mind you asking! Us hamsters are rather busy. We have toilet rolls to crawl through..."

"It won't take long! If Betsy is so bananas about gerbils, and, let's face it, who can blame her – we are beautiful beyond words – why on earth would she own an ugly old hamster?"

Hartley the hamster fumed. "Of course, how would you know this, being a thick gerbil, but Betsy's true love was always hamsters..." he began.

"And then she got you and changed her mind?" sneered Gerald.

Hartley's fur stood up on end in **fury.** "If you will excuse me, I am going to spray some hamster widdle right next to your cage!"

Now it was Gerald's turn to be **outraged.**

"And, if you will excuse me, I am going to lay a gerbil pellet right next to YOUR cage!"

THIS WAS WAR!

Now the pair of world's **best** pets had turned into the world's **worst** pets!

Hartley the hamster stuffed seeds in his mouth before shooting them one by one at the gerbil.

POW! POW! POW!

"OUCH!"

Gerald responded by squirting water from his bottle all over the hamster.

SPLOOSH!

"URGH! I'M ALL WET!"

Next Hartley squished down his toilet-roll tunnel so it would fit through the bars of the cages. Then he poked Gerald bang on the bottom with it.

POKE! POKE!

"OOF!"

This enraged Gerald, who climbed inside his see-through wheely ball, made it roll as fast as he could, then rammed it right at Hartley.

KERBANG!

"HELP!"

Hartley responded by leaping on his big wheel. It spun faster and faster to create a whirlwind. The whirlwind was so fierce it launched the little gerbil into the air.

WHIRR!

"NOOOOO!"

Things were escalating fast. Next Gerald used his
hammock as a catapult and fired nuts at the hamster.

TWANG!

"ARGH!"

Hartley then pressed his bottom up against the bars of
his cage, pointing it at Gerald. Then he blew off loudly.

PFFFT!

**"I ALWAYS KNEW HAMSTERS WERE
DISGUSTING,"** cried the gerbil, **"BUT THAT
TAKES THE BISCUIT!"**

Gerald leaped into action. Feeding his long tail

through the bars of the cages, he tickled the hamster with the tip.

TICKLE! TICKLE! TICKLE!

"OOH! HOO! STOP! STOP!"

Hartley responded with fire and fury. He placed his legs through the bars of his cage and pushed against the wall.

HEAVE!

This in turn shoved Gerald's cage along the side table.

SCRAPE!

"NO! NO!" begged the gerbil, seeing that his cage was about to topple to the floor.

HEAVE! repeated Hartley, pushing

further this time.

SCRAPE!

"PEACE! I WANT PEACE!" pleaded Gerald. He used a white tissue from his bedding as a flag of surrender. "I SURRENDER!" he cried.

Still the hamster kept pushing.

HEAVE!

The gerbil's cage balanced precariously on the edge of the table.

TWUNG!

Next, Hartley scuttled over to the other side of his cage. The two rodents were nose to nose.

"Don't do this, Hartley!" said Gerald.

"Why ever not?"

"Because us gerbils will take revenge! We will rise up in our hundreds, I mean thousands, I mean millions, I mean billions, I mean trillions! Then we will destroy hamsters once and for all!"

"I am so sorry," replied Hartley, "but you gerbils are beyond boring! Goodbye forever!"

With that, the hamster pushed one of his toes against the bars of Gerald's cage. It was the tiniest effort, but just enough to send the gerbil's cage flying.

"NOOOOOOOOOOOOOOOOOOOOOOOOOOOOOO!" cried Gerald in mid-air.

It was as if time sped up and slowed down all at once as his cage fell to the floor.

CLLLAAANNNGGG!

The cage hit the ground so hard that it broke into pieces.

CRUNCH!

The force of the impact sent the gerbil soaring.

WHIZZ!

"AAAHHH!"

Gerald landed on the floor with a **THUD!**

"HA! HA!" mocked the hamster from above as his arch-enemy lay there.

"Why are you laughing?" demanded Gerald.

"Because it's funny!" replied Hartley. The hamster then let out a booming theatrical laugh, like the villain in a pantomime. **"HA! HA! HA!"**

"What is funny," began Gerald, "is that you have unwittingly set me free! Now I can terrorise you!"

The hamster's eyes bulged with DEEP FEAR

as Gerald climbed up the curtains.

Hartley scurried inside his little house to hide.

Just then he heard the clang of someone landing on his cage.

CLANK!

"Little hamster! Little hamster. Let me in! Let me in!" began Gerald.

"Actually, hamsters are bigger than gerbils!" shouted Hartley from under the bedding in his tiny house.

"NO?" replied Gerald. "You say NO?"

"But I am not a pig, and you are not a wolf!"

"Just say it!"

"No! No! No! Not by the hairs on my chinny chin chin!"

"Then I'll huff, and I'll puff, and I'll blow your house down!"

"As if a silly little gerbil could blow over a house."

"I never said I would do it with my mouth!" said Gerald.

The next thing Hartley heard was the sound of a trumpet.

HOOO!

It was Betsy's!

Gerald was blowing through it with all his might.

The wind blew over Hartley's house with ease.

SHUNT!

The hamster was lying on his back with his legs waggling in the air, covered in sawdust.

Now it was the gerbil's turn to laugh villainously.

"HA! HA! HA!"

But Gerald had only just begun. He took some string from Betsy's desk. Next, he looped it through the top bars of the hamster's cage.

"What are you doing?" demanded Hartley.

"You will see, hamster!"

The gerbil leaped on to the lamp dangling in the centre of the bedroom.

Then he began swinging to and fro on the lamp until it took the cage with it.

"NOOOOOOOOO!" cried Hartley as he and his cage were swung through the air. "PLEASE! I HARDLY DID A THING TO YOU! SHOW ME MERCY!"

"AS IF I WOULD!"

Gerald swung the cage so hard that the string snapped.

TWANG!

The hamster cage hit the bedroom wall...

BASH!

...before exploding into pieces on the floor.

KERWALLOP!

"HA! HA!" laughed the gerbil from the lamp when he saw Hartley spread over the carpet.

"I wouldn't laugh if I were you!" began the hamster.

"Why is that?"

"Because I am free now too!"

Hartley leaped up, climbed the curtains and jumped on to the lamp.

"Now," said the hamster, "prepare to be crushed!"

There followed an

EPIC BATTLE!

When Betsy and her parents returned home at the end of the day, they discovered to their HORROR that their family home and everything in it had been...

DESTROYED!

The pair of rodents were caught red-handed speeding at each other on roller skates, jousting with chopsticks.

Father was furious. "WHAT THE BLAZES?"

Mother burst into tears. "WAH!"

Poor Betsy felt as if it were all her fault.

"I'm so sorry!" the little girl blubbed.

She scooped the rodents off her roller skates and held one in each hand. They tried to carry on poking each other with their chopsticks, but Father snatched those from them.

"Betsy!" he demanded. "Did you let your pets out of their cages?"

"NO!" said the girl.

"Then Hartley and Gerald must have broken out!"

The pair of naughty pets tried to look as sweet and innocent as possible, but this time it wasn't washing!

"Whatever are we to do with them?" asked a worried-looking Mother.

"They can't possibly stay here!" said Father.

"I think I know what could keep them both in order," replied Betsy.

The very next morning, Father kept an eye on Hartley and Gerald while Betsy took her mother back to **Chomp's Pets.** It took a great deal of pleading to persuade Mrs Chomp. Finally, she agreed to part with her precious Gigi. The giant guinea pig was now Betsy's!

The hamster, the gerbil and the guinea pig lived together in a brand-new super-strong cage.

To keep the warring pair of rodents in check, Gigi sat on them.

SQUISH!

"This is all your fault!" wailed Hartley.

"No, it's all YOUR fault!" whined Gerald.

"BOTH OF YOU, SHUT IT!" shouted Gigi as she greedily munched their entire stash of nuts.

CHOMP! CHOMP!
CHOMP!

The hamster and the gerbil lived unhappily ever after.

The Burgling BUDGIE

TWEET

TWEET

AND AGAIN, TWEET

The Burgling
BUDGIE

ONCE UPON A TIME, at the top of the tallest block of
flats, lived an elegant elderly lady all **alone.** From so
high up, the only living things Miss Havisham saw were
the birds perching on her windowsill. She grew to *love*
those birds and would talk to them.

"Good day, my little darlings!"

"How do you do?"

"You are looking more beautiful than ever!"

Every morning, she would sprinkle some breadcrumbs on the windowsill for them. However, a greedy one-eyed magpie would steal them all, gobbling down every last crumb.

"SQUAWK! SQUAWK! SQUAWK!"

Over time, Miss Havisham's friends, the birds, stopped coming. They lived in fear of the one-eyed magpie. Poor Miss Havisham felt rather lonely. But one day she awoke with a splendid idea. For the first time in her long life, she would own a pet!

So, as soon as she was dressed, immaculately as usual, with her hair styled in an elegant do, she set off. Miss Havisham danced all the way down the hundreds of stairs and skipped to her nearest pet shop, PICKWICK'S PETS.

Little did Miss Havisham know that waiting there for her was one of the world's very **worst** pets.

"A budgerigar?" asked the pet-shop owner. He was a round man called Mr Pickwick who wore a blond toupee on the top of his head. Cats, rabbits, hamsters, gerbils and even tropical fish were dotted around his shop. A little sausage dog lay by his feet. The dog had a sign on it that read:

"Are you sure you want a budgerigar, madam?"

"Yes!" replied Miss Havisham in her posh voice, her bright eyes flashing with excitement. "I would love a pet I can talk to and that will **talk back.**"

"Well, this one definitely talks back," he muttered.

"GRRRRR!" agreed Dickens the dog.

"I beg your pardon, Mr Pickwick?" asked Miss Havisham.

"Nothing, madam!" he fibbed. "I just said 'this one talks'. Now, madam, **you are in luck!** I have one last budgie in the shop!"

Mr Pickwick reached up to the top shelf behind him and brought down a birdcage, which he placed on the counter.

SHONK!

Inside the metal cage was the sweetest-looking bird. Budgerigars are tiny parrots that are a little bit green, a little bit yellow and a little bit blue. This one hopped around its cage.

CLINK! CLINK! CLINK!

Miss Havisham fell in *love* in an instant.

"Oh! He's absolutely adorable!"

Dickens the dog shook his head violently.

WOBBLE!

"May I be so bold as to enquire after the price?" asked Miss Havisham.

"Ten pee?" replied Mr Pickwick hopefully.

"TEN PEE?" repeated Miss Havisham, incredulous.

"All right, then, five pee!"

"Five pee for a budgie?"

"I like you, madam. Here, we have a special offer on budgies today. This one is two pee!"

"Two pee?"

"All right, you drive a hard bargain! Let's call it one pee!"

Before Mr Pickwick could change his mind, Miss Havisham whipped out her purse and slammed a one-pence coin down on the counter.

SHOINK!

"I should pay you to take him away!" muttered Mr Pickwick.

"Sorry, my hearing isn't what it was!"

"Nothing, madam! Meet Bumble. Bumble, meet your new owner!"

As soon as Bumble opened his tiny beak, the most surprising sound came out. He had a voice that was deep and gravelly, as if it belonged to a Salty old sailor.

"I don't like the look of her!" said Bumble.

Dickens the dog put his paws over his ears.

"What did Mr Bumble say?" enquired Miss Havisham.

"I didn't hear anything!" lied Mr Pickwick. "Did you?"

"Listen, mate, I ain't goin' home with that posho!"

"Sorry! I didn't quite catch that, Mr Bumble!" said Miss Havisham.

"Bumble said he can't wait to see his new home."

"NO! I DID NOT!"

protested the bird.

"Come on, little one, let's get going," trilled Miss Havisham. Her tone of voice couldn't have been more comforting. She lifted the cage off the counter.

"You'll pay for this, Wiggy!" protested the budgie. As he was hoisted through the air, he pushed his beak through the bars of the cage and bit on to Mr Pickwick's toupee, whipping it from his head.

WHISK!

"GRRRR!" growled Dickens, leaping to his master's defence.

"OH MY!" cried Mr Pickwick, slapping his hands on to his bald head.

Miss Havisham took the toupee out of the bird's beak and handed it back to the pet-shop owner. "I believe this belongs to you, Mr Pickwick!"

"I didn't even know I wore a toupee!" he fibbed, slapping it back on his bald head.

"Farewell!" called out Miss Havisham as she left **PICKWICK'S PETS** proudly with her new budgie. She and Mr Pickwick shared a warm smile.

Dickens the dog let out a gigantic sigh of relief.

"HUH!"

"Don't worry, Dickens! You will never see that budgie again! I promise you!" said Mr Pickwick.

The bird muttered with **discontent** all the way along the street, and all the way up the hundreds and hundreds of steps that led to Miss Havisham's opulently furnished flat.

"WHAT A NIGHTMARE!" declared Bumble on seeing the brightly coloured place for the first time.

"Mr Bumble! Welcome to your new home!" chirped Miss Havisham as she set the cage down softly on her grand piano. "I think you will be very happy here, with me as your new mama!"

"I was happy with Picknick! Whatever his name was!"

"Now, let Mama give you something to eat, little Mr Bumble!"

"Oi! Less of the little! I'm big for a budgie!"

"Would you care for some **scrumptious** cake?"

"CAKE! Now you're talking! But I don't want one of your homemade nightmares – I want something from a shop!"

Miss Havisham disappeared into the kitchen and came back into the living room with a cake box.

"Thank goodness for that!" said Bumble.

The old lady cut herself a slice, and then put some crumbs on to another plate for her pet.

"Here you go, Mr Bumble – some for Mama and some for you!"

Bumble banged his head against the bars of the cage.

"Oh! Silly Mama!" she said, and opened the hatch to let him out. Miss Havisham picked him up and gave him a little peck on his beak.

"MWAH!"

"PUKE!" exclaimed the budgie as he wriggled free.

"I beg your pardon, Mr Bumble?" asked Miss Havisham.

"What?"

"I thought I heard you say something."

"No," replied Bumble. "I can't talk."

"Oh," said Miss Havisham, baffled.

Bumble hopped down and over to the plates.

DINK! DINK! DINK!

The bird took one look at his crumbs,
and one look at her slice. Then he gobbled
up her slice in seconds, before letting out
the loudest, deepest burp.

"BURP!"

"Oh!" said Miss Havisham, shocked. "Mama had no idea
you were so famished!"

Then Bumble hopped over to the box and gobbled down
the entire cake.

"BURP!" he burped again,
incredibly loudly this time.

The sound was positively

BURPTASTIC.*

Miss Havisham pulled a

disapproving face.

* A real word you will find in the world's most trusted book, the
Walliamsictionary.

This was **not** the sound she'd hoped her pet
budgie would make. "Naughty Mr Bumble!"

This was just the beginning.

Soon Bumble was running **riot** all over Miss
Havisham's elegant flat. The budgie would...

...do loop-the-loops around the living room...

WHOOP!

...dive-bomb Miss Havisham while she was having
her afternoon snooze on the sofa...

"ZZZZZ! ZZZZZ!"

BOSH!

...turn the taps in the bath from hot to cold
so when Miss Havisham lowered herself in,
her bottom would go **bright blue**...

"OOOOOOOHHHHHH!"

84

...shred the silk curtains with his sharp talons...

RIP! RIP!

...play the grand piano in the middle of the night by

hopping from key to key...

DA! DE! DO!

(Poor Miss Havisham would wake up believing she was

being haunted by a musical ghost!)

...peck at Miss Havisham's pillows to fill her

bedroom with a **blizzard** of feathers...

PECK! PECK! PECK!

...flush the toilet while Miss Havisham was sitting on it...

SPLOOSH!

"OOOH!"

...and, worst of all, poop-bomb the antique rug!

KAPLOP! KAPLOP! KAPLOP!

Bumble was one bad budgie. But the bird's behaviour became **worse** when one frosty morning the one-eyed magpie landed on Miss Havisham's windowsill. The black-and-white creature was no doubt looking for more breadcrumbs. However, on spotting Bumble, the magpie tapped his beak on the glass to get the budgie's attention.

TAP! TAP! TAP!

"Oi!" he hissed to Bumble. "OI!"

The budgie was busy scoffing all the fudge from Miss Havisham's tin. The old lady was oblivious, reading a poetry book while reclining on her chaise longue.

"Bog off!" hissed Bumble.

"Nah! I am not bogging off!" replied the magpie. "Let me in!"

"I am **not** letting a dirty old bird like you in!"

"Let me in, I say!"

"Why should I? Eh? Tell me that!"

"Got a little business proposal for you! If you know what I mean?" The magpie winked.

"Is there something wrong with your one good eye?" asked Bumble.

"No. I am winking because I duck and I dive. I'm a bit tasty. I'm a mover and shaker, if you know what I mean?"

"You do what?"

"Us magpies, we steal, don't we?"

"Do you?"

"Everyone knows that," replied the magpie. "And I know you steal too."

"I NEVER!" snapped an outraged Bumble.

"Don't be daft, sunshine! I seen you through this window! Now let me in or I'll SQUAWK and SQUAWK and SQUAWK and tell the old dear everything you're up to!"

"You wouldn't dare!" replied Bumble, clearly concerned. His eyes flicked to Miss Havisham still happily reading away and not catching a word of this.

"I would dare! Now, open the window!"

Reluctantly, Bumble did as he was told. The budgie hopped on the handle, pushed it down and then with his beak he slowly prised the window open.

The magpie grinned and hopped into the flat.

"Me name's Magwitch," he said. "Magwitch the magpie."

"Bumble the budgie."

Magwitch stretched out his filthy black wing. After some consideration, Bumble shook it.

"Now tell me this, Bumble, do you wanna be rich?"

"Of course I do! Then I can get far away from the old dear!" he said, indicating Miss Havisham with his wing.

"Did you know the old dear's got a box stuffed full of jewels?"

"Has she?" asked Bumble.

"Not as **SHARP** as me, are you? I been spying on her through the window. She keeps 'em hidden under her bed."

"I never looked there."

"I know. I been spying on you too! So, what do you say we relieve her of them? If you know what I mean?"

"What?"

"Nick 'em!"

"Then what?"

"We'd sell them on to a gang of pigeons, they give them to a mob of hawks, they take them to a flock of seagulls. **BOOM!**

Then the jewels will be flown over the sea and sold abroad. Before you can say **'SQUAWK!'** we will be rich! All the birdseed you could ever dream of."

"I can dream of a lot of birdseed."

"Me too."

"Why do I have to cut you in, Magwitch? I could steal it all myself."

"You spent your whole life in some crummy pet shop waiting for some poor soul to buy you. I am on the street. I got the contacts in the bird underworld, don't I? We can split the birdseed right down the middle. Half and half. **Seventy/thirty.**"

"Budgies aren't stupid!" replied Bumble. "That's not half and half!"

"You drive a hard bargain! All right, then! **Eighty/twenty!**"

"Done!"

"You have been!"

So, the wicked pair set about their plan. As soon as night fell, and Miss Havisham was tucked up in bed asleep...

"ZZZZ! ZZZZ! ZZZZ! ZZZ!"

...Magwitch and Bumble fluttered around the top-floor flat, stealing anything that looked **valuable.**

Soon they had quite a haul.

Not just all the jewellery from the box under the bed but also...

A **porcelain** clown

A **gold** carriage clock

A **GLASS** elephant

A **brass** tray

A crystal decanter

Silver picture frames

A **radio**

Even the
electric kettle.

After all that flying around, picking up things and dropping them into Miss Havisham's old hatbox, the pair were spent.

As the silvery moon glowed outside the window, the budgie and the magpie hopped down on to the sofa.

"I'm pooped!" said Magwitch.

"Me too!" added Bumble.

"Well, let's have a little something to celebrate, before we make our escape."

That little something turned out to be a rather big something. They devoured a whole rhubarb crumble that Miss Havisham had bought for her dinner.

MUNCH! MUNCH!

Then the birds started on the biscuits, devouring packet after packet after packet.

CRUNCH! CRUNCH!

Finally, they started on Miss Havisham's giant tin of Christmas chocolates. They finished them all, even the coffee-flavoured ones.

Now the birds had eaten so much that they'd ballooned to the size of footballs. But the greedy pair weren't stopping there.

"After all that grub, I'm parched," said Bumble.

"Me too!" agreed Magwitch.

In the mood for celebration, they set their sights on a magnum of vintage champagne which stood on the sideboard. Working together, they eased the cork from the bottle and began guzzling the sparkling wine.

GLUG! GLUG! GLUG!

In no time, the pair were feeling quite **tipsy**, and more than a little **gassy.** All those bubbles in the bubbly had **ballooned** their tummies. Soon they found themselves being shot around the living room by their own bottom bangers.

PFFT!

"HELP!" cried Bumble.

PFFT!

"STOP!"

yelped Magwitch.

But they couldn't stop. They bounced around the opulent flat like rubber balls.

BOINK!

BOINK!

BOINK!

BOINK!

All this noise woke up Miss Havisham.

"WHO IS THERE, PLEASE?" she shouted from her bedroom.

"I can hear trumping!"

When she rushed into the living room, her nose

crinkled and she cried, "I CAN SMELL TRUMPING TOO!" Miss Havisham went to the window and opened it to let the awful stink out. Then she turned on the light in the room.

CLICK!

"Quick, let's get out of here!" hissed Magwitch.

"Don't forget the loot!" replied Bumble, really getting into the role of burglar now.

The birds bounced over to the hatbox. They seized a ribbon each with their beaks.

"What the **blazes** are you doing with my hatbox?" exclaimed Miss Havisham.

Then she realised that the huge, round, green, yellow and blue thing holding on to one side was actually Bumble.

"Mr Bumble? Is that you? How could you steal from your dear Mama?" she said, grabbing hold of her hatbox.

"I can feel a huge blast of gas coming!" said Bumble.

"Me too!" replied Magwitch.

"And this is a big one!"

"I know!"

"Three, two, one!"

Then together they cried, "BLAST OFF!"

PFFT!

And blast off they did!

The gas propelled the pair and the hatbox they were holding off the floor and through the window.

WHOOSH!

Poor Miss Havisham was still holding on.

"STOP!" she yelled.

The gas shot out so fast that the birds lost their grip on the box of loot.

They zoomed high into the night sky, hurtling towards space.

It was as if the solar system had become a GIGANTIC

PINBALL MACHINE!

Soon the two wicked creatures found themselves hurtling towards the hot, hot Sun!

WHOOSH!

Meanwhile, back on Planet Earth, Miss Havisham and her hatbox full of loot were falling through the air.

WHOOSH!

"HELP!" she cried.

But who could help her now?

As luck would have it for her, but bad luck would have it for them, on the ground below her Mr Pickwick the pet-shop owner was walking Dickens!

"LOOK OUT!" shouted Miss Havisham.

Mr Pickwick looked up to the sky...

BOSH!

...just as Miss Havisham fell on top of him.

"ARGH!"

Meanwhile, the box of
loot landed on Dickens.

BASH!

"HOWL!"

Everything went flying, including Mr Pickwick's toupee!

"Oh, my poor dear Mr Pickwick! Are you badly
injured?" asked Miss Havisham as he held her in his
arms.

"Nasty **bump** on my head," he said, rubbing it.
"Ouch! Are you all right?"

"I do believe you **saved** my life, Mr Pickwick!" she
exclaimed, tears in her eyes.

"If you need a refund on that budgerigar—" he began.

"No! No! No! Don't be silly, Mr Pickwick. Now, how is that delightful dog of yours?"

"MY POOR DICKENS!" sobbed the man.

She lifted the box, setting the sausage dog free.

To say thank you, Dickens gave Miss Havisham a big lick on the nose.

SLURP!

"Oh! Bless you!" spluttered Mr Pickwick. "You are a good woman, Miss...?"

"Amelia. Please call me Amelia," she replied softly, holding his gaze.

Mr Pickwick smiled, and Miss Havisham smiled back. These were smiles that hinted at romance.

Soon, the pair were meeting for walks in the park. Over time, the friendship between Miss Havisham and Mr Pickwick blossomed into **love.** The pair spent the rest of their days together.

Miss Havisham never felt lonely again.

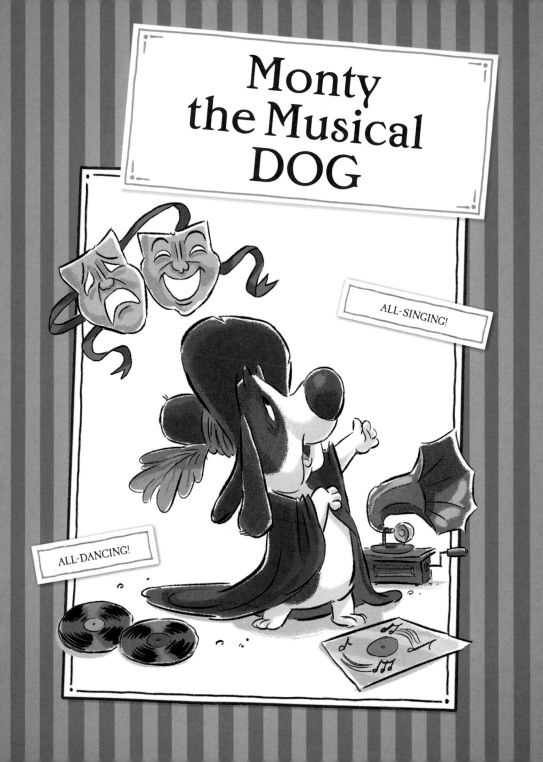

Monty
the Musical
DOG

MONTY WAS A DOG who enjoyed the **finer** things in life:
a morning bath complete with **bubbles**...
roast beef for dinner served in a silver bowl...
his **own** wicker basket lined with a soft tartan
blanket on which to sleep.

Monty was a basset hound. The much-loved pet lived in a grand old country house with a grand old dame. This grand old dame had a lifelong passion for musicals. In her younger days, Dame Emerald had been a **superstar** of musical theatre. She trod the boards of the West End in London and Broadway in New York. Dame Emerald knew every single word to every single song from every single show. She had an immense collection of records of all the classic musicals. She played them on her old-fashioned gramophone at full blast, singing along and reliving her glory days.

"LAH!"

As Monty heard musicals all day, every day, he grew to love them as much as his keeper. The pet would raid Dame Emerald's dressing-up box to act out scenes from the shows as the crackly old records spun round on the gramophone.

Monty would become the PHANTOM OF THE OPERA himself! For this he would don a mask, hat and cape.

Or he would put on a nun's habit! Then he would spin around playing Maria from **The Sound of Music.**

His favourite was to play the cold-hearted Javert from **Les Misérables.** For this, Monty would sport a long police-officer's coat and one of those funny sideways hats. When Monty really lost himself in a character and **howled** along to the show tunes, he would be mercilessly mocked. That's because Dame Emerald had another pet in her country pile: a black-and-white cat named Snipe. As is tradition in the animal world, the cat and the dog were sworn **enemies.** In the lounge of the house, Snipe would crouch on the headrest of Dame Emerald's armchair. This was somewhere Monty with his little legs could not reach. The cat would wait until the old lady dozed off with a glass of her favourite tipple in her hand. Then, from her place of safety, she would **snipe** at Monty.

"You can't sing a note, you **pongy** old pooch!" she purred.

"You don't know the first thing about musical theatre, you rotten old moggy!" Monty retorted. "I know the words to **every** song from **every** show!"

"Nonsense!"

"It is **not** nonsense!"

"Nonsense!"

"Not nonsense!"

"Well then, why, oh why, do you never sing the songs from this, **my** favourite show?" With that, Snipe leaped up on to the highest shelf of the cabinet and pulled out a black record with the word **CATS** in huge white letters on it.

The dog **fumed.**

Steam came out of his ears.

His eyes crossed.

"CATS! A MUSICAL?" he spluttered. "What sorcery is this!"

"It's not sorcery! It is **real!**" replied the smug-looking cat. "The old dear

never plays it because she knows it will hurt your poor ickle feelings!"

"As if my feelings would be hurt by a silly show about cats!" snapped Monty, tears welling in his droopy eyes.

"Then why are you crying?" sniped Snipe.

"I am not crying! I just have something in my eye!" he lied.

"A likely story, you lying hound! And it's not a silly show – it is one of the greatest musicals of all time, written by a genius composer so famous he's known simply as *The Lord*'!

CATS: THE MUSICAL has been wildly successful. Ran for decades. Seen by billions of people. And do you know why?"

"No, but I have a deep sense of dread that you are about to tell me, Snipe!" replied Monty.

"People love cats!" proclaimed Snipe.

"NONSENSE!" thundered the dog.

"NOT NONSENSE!"

"NONSENSE OF THE MOST NONSENSICAL ORDER! People love dogs more!"

Snipe's eyes narrowed. "If that were true, Monty, why would there be a **CATS: THE MUSICAL** and not a **DOGS: THE MUSICAL?**"

The dog fell silent. There was no answer to that.

"And there never, ever, ever will be a **DOGS: THE MUSICAL,**" continued the cat. "Do you know why?"

"Please continue!"

"Because," began Snipe, "dogs are **dirty, SMELLY** and **sniff** each other's bottoms!"

"How dare you? When we **sniff** each other's behinds, we are just saying hello!" protested Monty.

"Well, that is disgusting!"

"I'll tell you what is disgusting!"

"Pray do tell!"

"Being a cat and boasting about cats having a musical! Snipe, I will show you!"

"Show me what, Monty?" purred the cat.

"That dogs can have their own musical!"

"Never in a million years."

"A million dog years?"

"No! A million proper years!"

"Just you wait!"

"I am waiting!" purred Snipe.

Monty growled. **"GRRR!"** He stormed out of the lounge, slamming the tall wooden door shut with his tail.

SHUNT!

Passing by the old-fashioned telephone in the hallway, he spotted Dame Emerald's leather-bound address book. This had the names, addresses and telephone numbers of all her friends, many of them from the world of **SHOW BUSINESS.** With his front paws, he began flicking through the book, wondering whether the genius composer of **CATS** might be in there.

BINGO!

There was his address!

Now all Monty needed was some daring dogs willing to join him on a dangerous mission!

So, the very next morning, on his walk in the park and far away from the prying eyes of that conceited cat, Monty went to work. Dame Emerald slumped on a bench and let her precious pooch off the lead.

"Go and play, Monty! There's a good boy!"

Monty smiled and scampered off to find his friends:

Polo the poodle,

Coco the cocker spaniel,

and Daffy the dachshund.

He greeted them all in the customary doggy fashion by sniffing each of their bottoms.

SNIFF! SNIFF! SNIFF! SNIFF! SNIFF!

Once they had all reminded themselves of whose bottoms were whose, Monty got down to business.

"Listen, please, dogs!" began Monty. "I need your help!"

"To do what?" yapped Polo.

"To restore the pride of dogs all over the world!"

"My goodness gracious me!" said a stunned Coco.

"Tell us more, Monty!" implored Daffy. "The whole story!"

So Monty did just that. Out of earshot of Dame Emerald, he told his three furry friends the entire saga. How there was a smash-hit musical of **CATS**, but not one of **DOGS**. Needless to say, the pooches were **outraged.**

"This is a disgrace!"

"An insult to dogs everywhere!"

"Cats will never let us forget this! We must act!"

"Splendid you feel the same way I do!" said Monty. "Let's meet here in the park at midnight tonight. We will find the home of *The Lord* and force him to write a musical about dogs. All those who are in favour, raise a paw!"

To Monty's delight, all three dogs raised their paws.

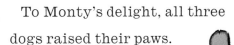

Later, under the cover
of darkness, the dogs
gathered. Once again, they **sniffed**
each other's bottoms to say hello. It would
be rude not to. But Monty was nowhere to be seen.

"Where is the old hound?" demanded Coco.

"He called us here in the dead of night!" moaned Daffy.

"I am going home!" declared Polo.

However, they heard a car engine far off. Headlights
flashed across the park.

"It's a trap!"

"It's the dog pound for us!"

"We're done for!"

As the car drew nearer, they spotted a familiar
face at the steering wheel. It was Monty!

"Hop in!" he said from the driving seat.

"Where did you get this?" asked Coco.

"It's my mistress's Bentley! Now get in
before she notices it's gone!"

The excited dogs all leaped in the back,
and the battered old car ROARED
off into the night's adventure.

They arrived at the tall brass gates of *The Lord's* castle in the early hours of the morning. To their great annoyance, the name of the residence was **CATS CASTLE**.

The dogs scaled the wall by all climbing on top of each other, making a ladder of dogs. Once inside the huge grounds, they scrambled up the turrets and located the master bedroom. As predicted, the legendary composer was fast asleep in his piano-shaped bed.

"ZZZZ! ZZZZ! ZZZZ!"

The dogs peered at him through the window. There were more cats than you could count in *The Lord's* bedroom. Cats on the carpet. Cats on the chaise longue. Cats curled up asleep on the bed. It was a **circus of cats!**

"I should have known *The Lord* was a cat person!" whined Monty.

"The **worst** kind of person!" added Polo.

"**Shush!** Let's be as quiet as we can so as not to wake him up!"

"DID YOU HEAR THAT, EVERYONE?" announced Daffy in far too loud a voice. **"BE QUIET!"**

"Shush!" shushed Monty.

"SHUSH!" repeated the dachshund.

"No. I meant you, Daffy!"

"Oh!"

Monty slid his long, slobbery tongue under the window, and slowly pushed it up. Now that it was open, he led his pack of dog commandos through.

"We need to get *The Lord* away from these nasty moggies!" he hissed. "You know how vicious they can be!"

Just as they were nearing the piano-shaped bed, Coco trod on a sleeping cat's tail.

"YEOW!" screamed the cat, waking all the others up.

"MIAOW!"

"HISS!"

The cats went bananas! Their sworn enemy – dogs – had broken into their master's bedroom.

The dogs all began barking.

"WOOF!"

"WOOF!"

"WOOF!"

This woke *The Lord*. He sat up in his bed. The world-famous composer was wearing red silk pyjamas, with

"THE LORD" sewn on to the pocket in black letters.

"ARGH!" he cried at seeing his bedroom full of dogs.

"WOOF!" **"WOOF!"** **"WOOF!"** barked the dogs.

The Lord leaped out of bed and fled down the hallway.

"HELP!" he screamed.

"AFTER HIM!" ordered Monty.

As the dogs gave chase, the cats raced after them.

They pinged out their razor-sharp claws...

PING! PING! PING!

...they bared their fangs...

"HISS!"

...and they thumped their tails hard on the floor.

THUMP! THUMP! THUMP!

One by one, the cats began launching themselves at

the dogs!

As you might expect of a zillionaire composer, *The Lord's* castle was full of priceless antiques: silk rugs, oil paintings, Venetian glass chandeliers, bronze busts and porcelain vases. All went...

CRASH! **BANG!**

WALLOP!

SMASH! THUMP!

...smashing on to the floor as the cats and dogs went to war.

Monty was out in front and could see that *The Lord* was getting away, **sliding** down the bannister in his silk pyjamas.

WHIZZ!
Monty took a running jump...

BOUNCE!
...and launched himself at *The Lord.*
The dog flew through the air...

WHIZZ!
...landing hard on the man's back.
DOOF!

He knocked *The Lord* on to his highly polished marble floor. So highly polished was it that as soon as his silk pyjamas made contact, he flew across it faster than a runaway train!

WHOOSH!

Monty stood on the man's back, riding him like a surfboard.

They slid along the hallway, straight into the music room, crashing into a grand piano.

TWONG!

"Ouch!" yelped *The Lord*.

Monty was thrown into the air...

WHIZZ!

...and landed with a **thud** on a pristine white sofa.

THOMP!

"No paws on the sofa!" shouted *The Lord*.

Being a good dog, Monty jumped off.

By this time, the other three dogs had caught up with them. They tumbled into the music room, cats swarming all over them.

Some were digging their claws into the dogs' backs.

TWANG!

Others were using their fangs to bite into the dogs' ears.

 **CRUNCH!**

Some were even thumping the dogs on the head with their tails!

THUD!

Others were doing all three!

TWANG! CRUNCH! THUD!

"I demand to know why there is a pack of dogs in my castle!" thundered *The Lord*.

There was no time to answer. The dogs had to fight back. They swung the cats round by their tails until they were nothing but a *blur*.

WHIRR!

And then they let go!

"MIAOW!"

There was more than enough room to swing a cat in the castle. The cats all bounced off the walls!

BISH! BASH! BOSH!

"STOP THIS MADNESS AT ONCE!"

bellowed *The Lord*.

All the animals stopped what they were doing and stood in silence. No one liked being told off by a *lord*.

"Explain yourself, dog!" he demanded, looking straight at Monty.

"Sir..." spluttered Monty.

"Lord!"

"Lord! May I just begin by saying I am a huge

121

admirer of your work..."

"Get on with it!"

"...but I was shocked to discover you have written a musical about cats, but not one about dogs."

"Well, cats are *magical* and mysterious," reasoned the composer. "And dogs, well, they sniff each other's bottoms."

The cats all sniggered. **"TEE! HEE! HEE!"**

"For goodness' sake, we are just saying hello!" thundered Monty. "Polo! Lock the door!"

The poodle did as he was told.

CLICK!

"What is the meaning of this?" spluttered The Lord. "I cannot be kept prisoner in my own castle!"

"Oh yes, you can! You are **not** leaving this room until you have written a musical about dogs!"

"Or what?" demanded The Lord.

"Dogs, what will we do?"

The dogs all took up places around the music room. It was packed full of awards. Each dog picked one up with their paws.

"Take your dirty paws off my Oscars, Tonys, Oliviers, Grammys and Emmys!" ordered *The Lord*.

"We will take a widdle on each and every one of your awards unless you write a show about us dogs!"

The Lord was so exasperated that it looked as if he were going to burst into tears.

The cats began stalking the dogs and **hissing.**

"Cats, back off! These dogs mean **business!**"

His pets arched their backs and retreated.

"Dogs! I **will** write your musical!" said *The Lord*.

"And put it on the stage!" said Monty.

"**No!** I will be a laughing stock!"

"Why?"

"Well," began *The Lord*, "I can't write **CATS: THE MUSICAL,** and then **DOGS: THE MUSICAL.** What's next? **HAMSTERS:** THE MUSICAL?"

"It could be a big hit with rodents!" reasoned Coco.

"NEVER! I AM A GREAT ARTIST!"

"Get to work, *Lord!*" ordered Monty. "Or your awards get it!"

Fortunately for a man who has composed 597 musicals in his lifetime, writing all the tunes on the grand piano came easily to *The Lord*. Soon there was song after song after song. Their titles were:

"Give Me Your Last Sausage!"

"SLURP, SLURP, SLURP FROM THE TOILET BOWL!"

"Barking up the Wrong Tree!" **"Slobber on the Window!"**

"If You Love Me, Then Tickle My Tummy!"

"I Will Sleep in Your Bed, and You Can Have the Basket!"

"Don't Blame Your Blow-off on Me!"

And, of course, the stand-out hit from the show, **"Sniffing Each Other's Bottoms"**.

There was one particular song that Monty had to force *The Lord* to write, or his Lifetime Achievement Award would be wazzled on. It was entitled simply, **"Cats Suck"!**

By dawn, the musical was finished.

"Fast work, *Lord!*" congratulated Monty.

"Actually, this one took me a lot longer than usual," replied the composer. "Next, I will book out one of my very own theatres in London's glittering West End, find a director, cast some actors and have the show up and running by the end of the month. Now, dogs, will you please get out of one of my many houses?"

"With pleasure. We will just take these awards with us for safekeeping!" said Monty, indicating for his fellow dogs to do so.

"NOOO!" said *The Lord*.

"You can have them back on the opening night! That way, we will know you are a man of your word."

"So be it! I will see you all at the first night of **DOGS: THE MUSICAL!**"

"HISS!" went all the cats, who were absolutely fuming!

*

125

A month later, the pack of dogs gathered outside the theatre as the great and the good arrived for the opening of the composer's latest masterpiece. Royalty. Film stars. Music legends. All were clamouring to get into the *Lord Theatre* to witness **DOGS: THE MUSICAL!** by *The Lord*.

At Monty's insistence, there was a sign outside the theatre that read: **ENTRY OF CATS IS STRICTLY FORBIDDEN!**

The four dogs, Monty, Polo, Coco and Daffy, all took their seats in the front row, two of them on either side of *The Lord* himself.

They were clutching his precious awards in their paws just in case he tried any **funny** business.

Dame Emerald happened to be in the audience among the famous faces, but she **dozed** off the moment the lights went down.

The orchestra struck up, and the **musical extravaganza** began. A single tear ran down Monty's cheek. He couldn't have felt **prouder.** At long last, dogs had their **own** musical, and, not only that, it had been written by one of the **greatest** composers of all time!

"Thank you so much, *my Lord!*" whispered Monty. "This is a night that will go down in dog history."

"Yes. Yes. Yes. Now, can I have my awards back?" pleaded *The Lord*.

"At the curtain call!" replied Monty.

"BAH!"

The show itself was lavish. It must have cost millions. Monty counted fifty actors on the stage, many of them legendary knights and dames of the theatre. All wore furry leotards with stuck-on tails. Their faces were painted with make-up so they looked like dogs. All fifty pranced around the stage singing, dancing and sniffing each other's bottoms.

The show went splendidly. The sets were **stunning,** the scene changes seamless and the lighting beautiful. What's more, the great composer had delivered one of his most memorable musical scores. Every song was a SHOWSTOPPER. The star-studded audience was devouring it like doggie chocs.

"BRAVO!"

"ENCORE!" "MORE!"

Then the closing number began, the one Monty had forced *The Lord* to write:

"CATS SUCK".

The words to the song went as follows:

Cats **suck**, don't you agree?
They leave hair all over the **settee!**
What other animal **licks** itself clean
And coughs up **fur balls** after they preen?
Let's get down to the **nitty gritty!**
Cats **aren't** nice and cats **aren't** pretty!
They are forever **moulting;**
It's utterly revolting.
They should all be **cursed**
As cats are the worst!

Monty was happily singing along to the song when he heard an all-too-familiar sound ringing in his ear.

"HISS!"

It wasn't just any old hiss. Oh no. Monty knew this hiss only too well. It was his archenemy! Snipe! The troublesome moggy had leaped on to the back of Monty's seat.

"Who dragged the cat in?" demanded Monty.

"I hid in Dame Emerald's fur coat," hissed Snipe.

"You are **not** welcome here!" thundered Monty. "Didn't you see the sign outside the theatre? Entry of cats is strictly forbidden!"

"Oh! I saw that, but cats make up their own rules. This **DOGS: THE MUSICAL!** is an absolute disgrace. Quite frankly, as a cat, I am disgusted!" sniped Snipe.

"Wonderful!"

"As is the entire cat community!"

"Purr-fect! Ha! Ha!" laughed Monty.

"Oh! It is purr-fect. Yes! Revenge will be sweet!" Monty looked alarmed. "Whatever do you mean, 'revenge'?"

"MY FELLOW CATS! ATTACK!" shouted Snipe.

All of a sudden, hundreds of cats appeared from beneath every coat, handbag and even wig in the theatre.

It was clear that all

this had been planned **perfectly.**

The cats launched themselves

at the actors on the stage.

WHOOSH!

"ARGH!"

"HELP!"

"NOOOOO!"

The cats destroyed the set by chewing it.

MULCH!

They ripped the red velvet curtains to

shreds with their razor-sharp claws.

RIP!

Worst of all, the cats even

ambushed the theatre usher

and stole all his tubs of

ice cream.

SLURP! SLURP! SLURP!

It was **pandemonium.**

Or **catdemonium!***

* See your **Walliamsictionary** for the full definition.

"ABANDON THE THEATRE! WE ARE UNDER ATTACK! CAT ATTACK!" shouted *The Lord* from the front row, wrestling his many awards from the bemused dogs and making his escape.

As the show's composer fled his own theatre, all the great and the good followed close behind. Except for Dame Emerald, who was still fast asleep.

"**ZZZZ! ZZZZ!**"

Now all that was left inside the theatre were the four dogs and hundreds of cats. The cats formed a circle round their enemies.

"The brave thing to do, my fellow dogs, is to stay and fight," began Monty, "but I feel, in this instance, the sensible thing to do is run away!

RUN AWAY AS FAST AS YOU CAN!"

That's exactly what they did. The dogs fled the theatre, the street and the whole of London's glittering West End, pursued by the army of cats.

"HISS!"
"WOOF! WOOF! WOOF!"

Back at Dame Emerald's country house, Monty was plunged into a waking nightmare. Every single night, Snipe waited for Dame Emerald to doze off on the sofa, and then blasted **CATS** from the gramophone. Snipe played the album so loudly that it could be heard in every room in the house, and even for miles around. Monty covered his ears with his paws and howled and howled and howled.

"YOOOO! YOOOOOOO! YOOOOOOOOOOOO!"

But nothing could drown out the sound of singing cats.

"TEE! HEE! HEE!" sniggered Snipe as she administered this terrible torture.

DOGS: THE MUSICAL! was a disaster. The show was forced to close after just one night. However, soon after, *The Lord* found his castle invaded by a thousand angry hamsters. They were furious that not only did cats have a musical but dogs did too, and they didn't. So, the poor composer had to go to work on a new show.

Strangely, **HAMSTERS:** THE MUSICAL! turned out to be a monster hit. The problem was that the guinea pigs were not happy. Nor the gerbils. And the rabbits were **furious.** Night after night, groups of angry animals broke down the door to *The Lord's* castle to demand he compose a show for them.

Soon, London's glittering West End was awash with *The Lord's* musicals about every single animal imaginable.

Bad
BUNNY

IF YOU HAD ONE of the world's worst owners, you
might become one of the world's worst pets. That was
the fate of a fluffy white rabbit called Houdini. She was
named after the greatest magician of all time, Harry
Houdini. Unfortunately, Houdini belonged to the direst

magician of all time, the Great Fiasco (although his real name was Colin).

The Great Fiasco was a shambles of a man, who looked as if he'd been dragged through a hedge backwards. He had a long, straggly moustache and wore a shiny purple suit, which gave him the appearance of a star in show business. Underneath the suit, he wore an old string vest, which rather shattered the illusion.

Like most children's entertainers, the Great Fiasco HATED children. The magician could be guaranteed to ruin any kid's party. By the end of every Fiasco performance, the birthday boy or girl would be in floods of tears, as the Great Fiasco would:

...slurp up all the jelly and ice cream...

GURGLE!

...snatch one of the grown-ups' watches to perform a disappearing trick and then **never** make it reappear...

SWIPE!

...scratch his bottom with his magic wand, then tap children on the head with it...

SCRATCH!

...hand the birthday boy or girl too many of his special gas-filled balloons so they would fly away...

WHOOSH!

...perform the famous magic trick of sawing a person in half – and then completely forget how to make it magic...

"ARGH!"

...sneeze while shuffling a pack of cards, then ask a child "to pick a card" when every single one was coated in snot...

"ATISHOO!"

...and, worst of all, Fiasco would YANK Houdini out of his top hat...

"YELP!"

For the Great Fiasco, the rabbit was just another prop. After racing home from that day's party on his purple motorcycle with Houdini in the sidecar, he would shove the rabbit back into her battered old hutch. The hutch was dark, cold and damp, having been wedged under the Great Fiasco's caravan for years. The Great Fiasco would ram a mouldy old carrot through the wire for the rabbit's dinner.

"There you go, you mangy old beast!" he'd shout. "Now, I don't want you waking me up in the middle of the night with your yelping! I don't care if the **foxes** come back! The Great Fiasco needs his beauty sleep!"

The **foxes** roamed the caravan park every single night. **Foxes** love nothing more than a nice juicy rabbit. But, paw as they might at the rabbit's cage, they just couldn't break in. Houdini would cower at the back, wishing she could make herself disappear.

Our story begins one Saturday afternoon, when the Great Fiasco had been booked to perform at another child's birthday party. Despite how awful he was, the magician did get work, as he was the cheapest children's entertainer in town. As was his way, Fiasco woke up hideously late and in a vile temper. The magician had

been up all night scoffing the giant birthday cake
he'd stolen from yesterday's party and now he
had a **TUMMY ACHE**.

"URGH!"

He stumbled out of his caravan,
instantly getting tangled up in his own underpants,
which were hanging on the washing line.

"GET OUT OF MY WAY, PANTS!"
he bawled.

"TEE! HEE! HEE!" sniggered Houdini.

Fiasco was furious at being laughed at.

He booted the rabbit's hutch.

TWONK!

"SHUT IT, YOU REVOLTING
CREATURE!"

"For goodness' sake, please
could you be more **kind**
to your rabbit?" called
out the nice old
lady from the
caravan
next door.

Her name was Babs. She was short for her age (seventy-five), but had a big mop of curly white hair that ensured she was always noticed. Babs was the **kindest** person in the caravan park by far. She always had a beaming smile for everyone.

"YOU CAN SHUT UP AND ALL, YOU OLD BOOT!" Fiasco shouted back.

"Charming!" huffed Babs.

"COME 'ERE, YOU!" said Fiasco as he reached his grubby hands into the hutch and yanked the rabbit out.

"ARGH!" squealed Houdini.

"DON'T YOU 'ARGH' ME!" he shouted.

Houdini had had enough. With her long, sharp teeth, she bit hard into the magician's hand.

MUNCH!

"OWEE!" he cried in pain. "BAD BUNNY!"

"Serves you right!" remarked Babs. "I hope it hurt!"

Fiasco was **furious.** He hurled his rabbit into the sidecar...

THWUNK!

...before taking off at speed on his motorcycle.

VROOM!

He headed straight for Babs!

"STOP, YOU FRUIT-AND-NUT CAKE!" she cried.

Still he kept on coming. *VROOM!*

Babs had to leap out of the way into a bush.

VROOM!

RUSTLE!

"HA! HA!" snorted Fiasco as he raced out of the caravan park, Houdini's ears flapping in the breeze. She looked back to see poor Babs clamber out of the bush.

When the pair skidded to a halt outside the house for the party, Fiasco gave his rabbit a **stern** talking-to.

"Now, I don't want any cheek out of you, you nasty little beast!" he said. Then he yanked her up from his sidecar before stuffing her deep into his top hat.

"YELP!" went Houdini.

"GET IN!"

She bit Fiasco bang on the nose.

MUNCH!

"OWEE!" he cried in pain. "BAD BUNNY! YOU CAN STAY IN THERE!" he said, pushing the rabbit deeper and deeper into the deep, **dark,** secret compartment in his hat.

SQUISH!

The Great Fiasco then put on his top hat. Next, he shambled into the party, a good few hours late.

As always, he had completely forgotten the name of the child whose birthday it was.

"Happy birthday, Susie!" he growled.

"My name is Freddie!" corrected the birthday boy.

"Tee! Hee!" sniggered Freddie's little brother Xander.

"Whatever!" barked Fiasco. "Now sit down, shut up and marvel as I pull a revolting rabbit from my hat."

However, try as he might, the Great Fiasco just couldn't get Houdini to come out!

Fiasco thumped the hat.

THUMP! THUMP! THUMP!

He shook it as hard as he could...

SHAKE!

...banged the hat on the table...

BOINK!

...threw it like a Frisbee...

WHIZZ!

...pushed his long moustache inside the hat, trying to tickle the rabbit out...

TICKLE!

...hurled the hat up into the air...

WHOOSH!

...poked his magic wand into the hat...

POKE! POKE! POKE!

...bellowed into it...

"HOUDINI! OUT! NOW!"

...stuck the hat on his head and jumped up and down on the spot...

BOING! BOING! BOING!

The Great Fiasco even did a GINORMOUS BOTTOM BANGER into his own top hat. He was sure that would smoke the rabbit out.

PFFT!

The brothers held their noses and looked over to their parents.

"I don't want him for *my* party!" cried Xander.

"He was the best in the price range!" replied his father as his mother shook her head.

"Never again! Please!" pleaded Freddie.

Sadly, the bottom banger didn't work. Houdini was not coming out! Well, not as Fiasco wanted. Instead,

Houdini, like her namesake – who was a brilliant escapologist – nibbled her way out of the top of the hat.

NIBBLE! NIBBLE! NIBBLE!

After all that waiting, the children were delighted to see the rabbit appear in the most **unexpected** way.

They **clapped** and cheered.

"HOORAY!"

The Great Fiasco was furious that the rabbit had stolen his thunder.

"BAD BUNNY! GET BACK IN THERE!" he bawled, shoving the animal into the hat. However, as Houdini had nibbled a hole, she fell right through it, landing on her bottom with a THUMP!

Houdini played up to the children, rubbing her sore bottom. Again, this made them howl with laughter.

"HA! HA! HA!"

Freddie and Xander were now rolling around on the floor, laughing so much their tummies hurt.

"HEE! HEE! HEE!"

The Great Fiasco was ENRAGED! He snatched the rabbit and marched her out of the party.

"Don't go!" called Freddie.

"This is hilarious!" added Xander.

"YOU NEVER, EVER, EVER UPSTAGE ME LIKE THAT, HOUDINI!" wailed the magician. "I AM THE

Great Fiasco AND DON'T YOU FORGET IT!"

With that, he hurled the rabbit into the sidecar.

THUNK!

"YELP!" yelped Houdini.

"SERVES YOU RIGHT!"

As the magician clambered astride the motorcycle, the rabbit seized her moment. She chomped as hard as she could on the man's bottom.

"YOWEE!" he screamed in pain, leaping up into the air. "BAD BUNNY! JUST WAIT UNTIL I GET YOU HOME!"

The Great Fiasco revved his motorcycle…

VROOM!

then raced off down the street.

WHIZZ!

He shouted at the rabbit all the way home. "HOW DARE YOU! I AM A SUPERSTAR MAGICIAN! I AM IN HUGE DEMAND FOR CHILDREN'S PARTIES WITHIN A ONE-MILE RADIUS! AND YOU ARE NOTHING BUT A PROP!"

Houdini knew she was much more than a prop. She had entertained those children at the party, and she was sure she could do it again.

The motorcycle flew through the gates of the caravan park they called home.

On spotting Babs putting her washing out, the Great Fiasco began speeding towards her again.

VROOOOM!

"ARGH!" she cried as she leaped out of the way of the motorbike, landing in a muddy puddle.

SPLOOSH!

"HA! HA!" snorted Fiasco, skidding to a stop outside his caravan.

"Come here, Houdini, you darling little thing," he said in a tone that alarmed Houdini because she could tell he was acting. "Let's put you in your lovely little hutch."

Then Fiasco did something he'd never done before. He left the door of the cage unlocked. "I hope those naughty **foxes** don't come and gobble you up during the night. Sweet dreams, my bunny wunny!"

Just as Houdini was about to make a hop for it, she saw the foxes appear out of the gloom.

"GRRRR!"

Their fangs glistened in the light of the moon. If Houdini didn't do something fast, she would be **fox** food.

Just within reach above the door to the cage was a giant pair of Fiasco's underpants. Houdini leaped up out of the cage and tugged the underpants off the line.

TWANG!

Then she slid them down in front of her and jumped up on to the caravan.

THE DISAPPEARING TRICK!

The **foxes** had no clue where the rabbit had gone. They ran off, chasing their tails.

"YAP! YAP! YAP!"

Houdini climbed to the top of the caravan. Now she wanted to get her own back on the far-from-Great Fiasco. From the roof, the rabbit could hear Fiasco splashing about in his tin bath below.

SPLASH! SPLOSH! SPLISH!

So she reached down, whisked the saw Fiasco used for magic tricks out of the motorcycle sidecar and, one by one, began sawing the outside edges of the caravan.

WAH! WAH! WAH! WAH!

A crowd of folk from the caravan park began to gather, eager to see what was going on. Houdini put her paw up to her lips so they would keep quiet.

"SHUSH!"

She would hate to ruin the surprise!

It was hard work, but soon the rabbit had sawed along each of the edges. Then, with just a nudge of her paw, the walls of the caravan collapsed.

BOOF! BOOF! BOOF! BOOF!

Like a magic trick, the Great Fiasco was revealed. The magician was sitting up in his tin bath in the nude!

Now everyone in the caravan park could see him!

The crowd pointed and laughed.

"HA! HA! HA!"

"DON'T FORGET TO WASH YOUR BOTTY!" called out Babs, who was laughing harder than anyone.

"HA! HA! HA!"

The magician looked up and saw Houdini perching on the branch of a tree. "YOU NASTY LITTLE FIEND! I WILL GET YOU, HOUDINI! I WILL GET YOU IF IT IS THE LAST THING I DO!" he bawled. Fiasco began to stand up to give chase, but, realising he wasn't wearing any clothes, plonked himself down in the bath again!

SPLASH!

"Pass me something to wear!" he shouted.

Babs picked up a pair of his slippers.

"There you go!" she chirped as she passed them to him, much to the amusement of everyone.

"HA! HA! HA!"

Now all that was left was for Houdini to make the Great Fiasco disappear forever. She scuttled down from the branch. Next, she grabbed one of the magician's hundreds of balloons from the sidecar. With all her might, she blew into it. Once it was **inflated,** she tied the balloon to the bath.

"What's that rabbit up to now?" asked an old man.

"I think I know!" replied Babs. "Come on, everyone, let's do what Houdini is doing!"

At once, everyone in the caravan park grabbed balloons and began blowing them up with gas from the magician's cylinder.

"OI!" shouted the Great Fiasco.

"WHAT ARE YOU DOING WITH MY BALLOONS?"

He was unable to get out of the bath.

He was nude! And only had a pair of

slippers to wear!

In no time, hundreds of balloons were

attached to the tin bath and it

lifted into the air!

"HELP!" cried the Great Fiasco

as he and his bath began

floating into the sky.

Everyone cheered to see the back of him.

"HOORAY!"

The Great Fiasco drifted up, up, up  into the air. Soon he was nothing more than a **dot** in the sky until he disappeared forever.

PING!

It was to be the Great Fiasco's **final** magic trick! The rabbit lifted her paw and waved goodbye for the last time to the nasty brute.

So, whatever happened to Houdini? Well, the rabbit became a full-time magician. Now she performs at children's parties under the name

HOUDINI THE BAD BUNNY!

Houdini's signature trick is pulling a **person** out of a top hat – none other than her glamorous assistant, **Babs!**

"TA-DA!"

The Secret Diary
of a
Supervillain's
CAT

 MONDAY

Dear Diary,

Would you believe I've been stuck in the pet-shop window for a **whole week**?

Oh! The noise! The animals! The waft of wee!

I had all but given up hope – woe was me! – when first thing this morning a *mysterious* bald man in a fetching beige evil-dictator suit waltzes into the shop. He immediately points at me. Who can blame him?

I, Candelabra, am by far the most beautiful fluffy white cat in the shop. If not the entire world!

"I lost my last moggy in an unfortunate accident in an underwater base," he says in an accent that is impossible to place. Russia? Switzerland? Birmingham?

"Accidents happen," mutters the pet-shop owner. He clearly hasn't been listening to a word the *mysterious* bald man has been saying.

"Does the cat **hiss?**" asks the bald man.

"Does it kiss?" asks the pet-shop owner, looking rather concerned.

"No, **hiss,** you fool! I need a good **hisser.**"

"A good kisser? I would strongly advise against kissing the cat, sir. You don't know where it's been!"

"No! **Hisser!**"

"Oh yes, Candelabra **hisses!** Look!" With that, the pet-shop owner yanks my tail, which he knows I loathe with a passion.

"**HISS!**" I hiss.

"I will take it!" says the bald man.

"It's one hundred quid. Cash!"

One hundred quid seems awfully cheap to me. I thought I would go for squillions! Well, the bald man has other ideas as he pulls out a laser gun and **ZAPS** the pet-shop owner.

ZAP!

"ARGH!"

The pet-shop owner disappears into thin air.

WHOOSH!

Well, I'm beginning to suspect this *mysterious* bald man is not as nice as he looks. And he doesn't look that nice!

"My name is Dr X," he says.

"And I am Candelabra!" I reply, reaching out a paw. We shake hands.

"Welcome to my evil world!" he says.

I smile weakly.

Dr X puts me in a solid gold cat box (very chic but bum-numbingly uncomfortable), and I am taken by helicopter (convenient but noisy) to a secret island (pretty but remote). The island rears out of the sea as we approach.

WHOOSH!

"Well, I never!" I say, although Dr X cannot hear me over the roar of the blades.

"WHAT?"

"WELL, I NEVER!"

"WHAT?"

"NEVER MIND!"

"WHAT?"

It turns out the island is the top-secret base of Dr X's top-secret criminal organisation, **XXX**. **XXX** specialises in extortion, blackmail and revenge. The people who work at **XXX** seem nice enough, though.

They while away the hours practising karate, wrestling and shooting flamethrowers at each other. I'm not sure what exactly they are practising for, but it looks **exhausting.** Not for me, dear. Thank goodness, being a cat, I'm not expected to join in!

Dr X takes me to his **secret lair** and puts an absolutely gorge diamond collar round my neck. (I shudder to think of the price, but I am **worth it,** babes.)

"Diamonds are forever," he purrs. "Unless you displease me."

"Why, thank you, Doc!" I say.

He then picks me up and places me on his lap.

"Candelabra, you are to sit here all day and **hiss** at anyone who angers me."

"HISS!" I hiss.

"Perfect," he purrs, before reaching into a fishbowl and pulling out a live **piranha,** which he feeds to me.

I must say I am **not** keen on the taste, but I swallow it like a good pet.

Before we know it, it's nighttime, and I go to sleep on

Doc's four-poster bed, thinking I might be the luckiest cat in the world.

Now, I know what you're thinking – cats can't hold pens, so how did you write this? I typed it, you fool!

🐾 TUESDAY

Dearest Diary,

Doc wakes up in bed with only one thing on his mind – an evil plan. It turns out he has had **many** evil plans over the years, though sadly none of them have ever been successful:

...Moving the Moon in front of the Sun to plunge the Earth into **eternal darkness...**

...Miniaturising Buckingham Palace so he could put it in his pocket and run off with it...

...Creating an army of **robot killer bananas** to destroy the planet...

...Stealing all the socks in

the world, creating a shortage, and then selling them back to people at a **hundred** times the price...

...Seizing control of the **weather** and threatening every country in the world with a *light drizzle* unless they give him a **trillion** dollars. And a bag of marshmallows...

...Unleashing upon the world a deadly swarm of **ladybirds...**

...Turning the entire population of the world into **cheese...**

...Holding the President of the United States's **underpants** for ransom...

...Taking over the world's TV stations and making **everyone** watch only **gardening** programmes for **all eternity...**

Over a cosy breakfast in bed – scrambled eggs for Dr X, a live **piranha** again for me (beginning to pine for a good old-fashioned tin of cat food) – the evil mastermind expounds on his latest plan.

"Candelabra, I am going to take over **the world!**" he begins.

"Ooh, good for you, dear," I reply, making the best of the live **piranha** as it flaps about in my gob.

"I have located a **giant volcano** that I am hollowing out!"

"I hope you got planning permission!" I say.

"Inside, I'm going to have a space-rocket launching pad and a monorail."

"Ooh! I've always wanted to go on a monorail! They have one at Legoland!"

"And **hundreds** of people working for me. All wearing boiler suits!"

"Not flattering, are they, boiler suits? They make you look like you have a **humongous** bottom! But do go on, Doc," I urge him.

"Then, Candelabra, with my **mega rocket,** I am going to hijack the spacecraft of all the major global powers. They will blame the hijacking on each other and threaten a world war!"

"Ooh! Not another one! That'll be the third!"

"Out of the ashes of the civilisation we know, I, Dr X, will finally fulfil my destiny, to **rule the world!**" he declares.

"Rule the world?" I say. "Seems like an awful lot of hard work! Not for me, dear!"

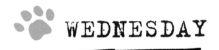

WEDNESDAY

Darling Diary,

Ooh, the glamour! No sooner have I woken up than my doc whisks me off on a private jet (not much leg room, but at least we didn't have to queue at the airport) to see how work is progressing on this brand-new **TOP-SECRET underground base** (you know, the one in the **volcano)**. The poor builders have been working day and night for weeks, trying to hollow the thing out.

"Candelabra, these are the new builders," says Dr X. "The old builders were too slow, so I **ZAPPED** them into oblivion!"

"A bit harsh, Doc!" I remark.

Then he consults the **TOP-SECRET** underground-base plans. "So, over there is going to be a pool," he says, pointing to a corner.

"Super!" I say. "A swimming pool?"

"NO! A pool of **piranhas!**"

My heart sinks. I am already sick to death of eating the blasted things. "I hate to be a party pooper, but how about a nice pool of cod or tuna or oak-smoked salmon?" I suggest with a smile.

"**NO!**" shouts Doc. My word, he's got a temper on him! Well, that's supervillains for you! "It has to be **piranhas!** What kind of self-respecting evil criminal mastermind has a pool of smoked salmon? It has to be crocodiles or sharks or **piranhas!**"

"All right! All right! Keep your hair on, dear," I say without thinking. OOPS! Dr X has a face like **thunder.**

"Is that meant to be funny, Candelabra?" he purrs menacingly.

"N-n-no!" I stammer.

"I would hate you to have some kind of 'unfortunate accident'."

The way he says 'unfortunate accident' makes me think it wouldn't be an accident at all, so I quickly change the subject.

"Do go on with your evil plan, please, Doc!" I implore.

"Over the top of the pool of **piranhas,** I will have a bridge."

"Ooh, lovely. Romantic stroll. Take in the scenery!" I say.

"A secret button on my desk will control the bridge."

"Oh dear," I say. "I think I know where this is going."

"If anyone displeases me, then I will simply press the button. A trapdoor in the bridge will open, plunging them into the pool of **piranhas.** SPLOSH! There they will be eaten alive!"

"Ooh! Sounds painful! Not for me, dear!" I reply.

"If you make any further comments about my baldness, then that is what will happen to you!" he says with an evil chuckle. "HA! HA! HA!"

Well, that made the atmosphere *frosty,* I can tell you!

THURSDAY

Dearest Darling Diary,

This morning Doc took me for a jaunt on the monorail,

which was perfectly pleasant. To be honest, it would have been quicker to walk from one side of the **volcano** to the other. I didn't dare mention it, though, because he still seems to be in a stinking mood about the builders. Everything is way behind schedule, and the space rockets he was planning to hijack in orbit are due to be launched any day now.

"This second firm of builders is even slower than the first!" he complains later in his **TOP-SECRET** lair. Lots of rocks and technology in there. Nice if you like that sort of thing. Not for me, dear!

"Should I hiss at them?" I suggest.

"No. I am going to have all the builders obliterated!" he says.

"A bit much!" I say, coughing up a fur ball.

Then he calls out, "Send the henchmen in."

Three frightening figures enter the **TOP-SECRET** lair.

First, there is a very tall man with all $silver$ teeth. (I imagine he never, $ever$ brushed his real teeth as a child.)

Then a stocky man with a bowler hat that can kill (sort of like a KILLER FRISBEE).

Finally, an old lady with daggers coming out of her shoes (not sure she bought the shoes on the high street).

"**HISS!**" I hiss.

"No! Don't **hiss** at them!" says Dr X. "These are MY henchmen! Now," he says to them, "I want you to eliminate all the builders."

The henchmen all nod and leave the lair. They don't smile much, but they seem nice enough.

FRIDAY

Dearest Darling Dearest Diary,

Well, it's all go being the cat of a criminal mastermind, I can tell you! A third firm of builders have been working on Doc's **volcano** and it is finally ready! TA-DA! They have even remembered to install a kitty litter tray for yours truly. It's a relief, as I haven't been for days!

But, just as I am about to do my business, a siren sounds.

WAH! WAH! WAH! WAH!

It's so loud that it puts me right off my poop. I don't know about you, but I need to poop in peace!

The siren is sounding because the huge metal ceiling of the **volcano** is sliding off. The top of the ceiling looks

like a lake, which is devilishly clever, though
painful for anyone diving in for a swim!

Ouch! Not for me, dear!

In the base of the
volcano, all the men in boiler suits run
around trying to look as busy as possible. I
notice they are just running around in circles
doing nothing. Well, I guess it makes sense to look
like you're working hard when being employed by an evil
criminal mastermind!

"Launch the **mega rocket!**" orders Dr X. Well I never,
he can sound so butch when he wants to!

So this great ugly thing, like a giant toilet-roll tube,
takes off from the base of the **volcano.**

VROOOM!

Flames from the rocket roar!

I can feel myself becoming hotter and hotter!

"MY WHITE FLUFFY FUR IS SINGED!" I cry.

"ABORT TAKE-OFF!"

"SILENCE!"

shouts Dr X.

"It's all right for you.

You've got no hair!"

OOPS!

Well, you could cut the atmosphere with a knife.

"Would you like to be bald?" he asks me.

"Ooh, not for me, dear!"

"The piranhas in my pool will have your fur off in a second!"

"If you will excuse me," I say, "I just need to finish some urgent business, of the bottom variety!"

Well, I have barely skulked back over to the litter

tray when the **mega rocket** comes back down again!

It lands in the base of the volcano with a smaller Russian space capsule inside. The cosmonauts are forced by the men in boiler suits to board the monorail. They complete one lap of the track and get off exactly where they got on! Pointless!

SATURDAY

Dearest Diary Darling,

Well, after the hair comment yesterday, me and Doc aren't speaking. Not a word! Awkward! So I slope off back to the litter tray for another go.

Just as I am lowering my white furry bottom on to the litter, the siren goes off again!

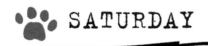

WAH! WAH! WAH! WAH!

Ooh! So loud! Not for me, dear!

The ceiling slides open and the **mega rocket** blasts back up into the air again! The men in boiler suits run around in circles again, pretending to be busy.

When I'm finally in the mood to poop, that blasted siren wails again! The **mega rocket** is back already, this time with an American space capsule inside. The astronauts are forced by the men in boiler suits to board the monorail. They do a lap and get off again.

Ridiculous!

I completely abandon my poop. Not for the first time. I pad over to Doc and leap on his lap.

"Well done, dear!" I say, trying to break the ice, but he doesn't speak to me.

"I have seen one of those astronauts before! I am sure of it!" he murmurs to himself.

Ooh, the drama!

🐾 SUNDAY

Diary Darling Dearest,

Well, get this! Dr X was right! One of those American astronauts **was** actually a legendary British secret agent called **006½** in disguise. He and the doc have major beef. Handbags at dawn!

The three henchmen march the secret agent to Dr X's lair, and they stand on the bridge. **006½** is placed right over the trapdoor! Cheeky!

I do my best to **hiss** at the secret agent. "**HISS!**" I say, but it comes out more like a purr. "PURR!"

I can't help it! **006½** is gorge, dear! Absolutely gorge! Tall and handsome with the most perfect smile. Everything Dr X isn't! No wonder he loathes **006½** with a passion!

It turns out the secret agent is on a secret mission to the secret base to find out the secret plan. Now, if I was his enemy, and he had foiled my plans for world domination time and time again, I think I would just pull out a gun and BANG! BANG! BYE-BYE! But oh no, my doc wants to drag it out. Silly, really.

"So, we meet again, **006½!**" he says.

"A hollowed-out **volcano!**" says the secret agent.

"The idea is positively explosive!"

006½ is just as funny as he is handsome!

"HA! HA! HA!" I laugh.

 "SILENCE!"

thunders Dr X. He squeezes me so hard I cough up a fur ball.

 BLURGH!

Not pretty.

"Excuse me, **006½!**" I say. "Dr X is just showing off because you are here."

"I AM NOT!" snaps Dr X.

"YOU ARE, DEAR!" I say. "It's not **006½'s** fault that he is so much handsomer and funnier and less bald than you!"

Well, this makes Doc fly into a rage.

"Into the **piranha** pool you go, Candelabra!" he shouts, and he picks me up and hurls me towards the water.

006½ leaps up and catches me in his arms.

"My hero!" I purr.

Then I can see Dr X reaching for the secret button on his desk. "JUMP!" I cry.

006½ leaps out of the way just in time.

The henchmen rush at him! Still holding me, **006½** dispatches them into the pool one by one with his superb combat skills.

SPLISH! SPLASH! SPLOSH!

"ARGH!"

"HELP!"

"NO!"

The three are eaten alive by **piranhas.**

CHOMP! CHOMP! CHOMP!

Now Dr X rises from his seat and takes out his laser gun.

"So long, pussycat!" says **006½,** hurling me at Dr X.

WHOOSH!

I land on Dr X's bald head.

THWACK!

With the end of my tail poking into his eyes, he can't see a thing, so **006½** rushes at him! The secret agent wrestles the laser gun from the doc, flinging it into the **piranha** pool.

PLOP!

In a rage, Dr X grabs me and chucks me off his head.

WHOOSH!

"MIAOW!"

I land with a thud on his desk.

Now **006½** and Dr X are fighting on the bridge.

The trapdoor has gone back up again by now, and the pair are *twirling* around it like ballroom dancers. I just need to pick the right moment to press the button.

Dr X has **006½** just where he wants him. Standing on the trapdoor.

"PRESS THE BUTTON NOW, CANDELABRA! NOW!" shouts Dr X.

But I am torn, dear. TORN!

"WHAT ARE YOU WAITING FOR?" he demands.

006½ is so smart he knows what is happening, so he spins his enemy round. Now Dr X is standing right over the trapdoor.

"NOW, PUSSYCAT, NOW!" shouts the secret agent.

I press the button and...

SPLOOSH!

...Dr X plunges into the **piranha** pool.

The supervillain is devoured in seconds.

"ARGH!"

"OOPS!" I joke.

CHOMP!

CHOMP!

CHOMP!

186

Just then **006½** yanks on the base's secret self-destruct lever on the wall of the lair.

BEEP! BEEP! BEEP!

"VOLCANO WILL EXPLODE IN ONE MINUTE AND COUNTING!"

says a robotic voice over the loudspeaker.

006½ turns to go.

"Aren't you taking me with you?" I implore.

"No. I hate pussycats," he says nonchalantly, "especially fluffy white ones! They hardly go with my macho image! That's why I have a poodle!"

"Well, I hate smug secret agents!" I snap back, just like that!

When he runs over the trapdoor on the bridge, I press the button on the desk.

SPLOOSH!

"ARGH!" cries **006½** as he too is devoured by **piranhas.**

CHOMP!

CHOMP!

CHOMP!

"VOLCANO WILL EXPLODE IN THIRTY SECONDS AND COUNTING!"

says the robotic voice.

Just then a gaggle of men in boiler suits rush into the lair.

"Where's Dr X?" they ask.

"Eaten by his own **piranhas!** Ooh, the irony! I did tell the boss to fill his pool with oak-smoked salmon, but would he listen?"

"So, who is in charge now?"

I look around. I am sitting behind Dr X's desk. It feels good.

"I am!" I reply. "I am going to board the **mega rocket** and blast off into space! I will destroy the world from there!"

Then I let out an evil laugh.

"HEE! HEE! HEE!"

Oh! This is for me, dear!

WHOOSH!

I fly off into space, and from all the way up there in the darkness I look down at Earth.

There is a big red
button on the control
panel of the **mega rocket.** It says:

DESTRUCT THE EARTH –
PRESS HERE.
HAVE A NICE DAY!

That must be the right one!
So I slap it with my little pink paw.
SLAP!
Then a gigantic **ZAP** of laser light flies from
the rocket to the Earth.

ZAP! KABOOM!

The Earth explodes into millions of pieces.
"HEE! HEE! HEE!" I let out my evil
laugh again.

Then I realise something. I am floating alone through space on the **mega rocket** with absolutely nowhere to go. I can't go back to Earth because I have destroyed it. I have run out of fuel and, worst of all, there isn't a single tin of cat food on board. Or any kitty litter, and I still haven't pooped!

I am doomed to be floating through cold, dark, empty space until the end of time. To be honest, **Dear Diary,** I feel a tiny bit silly.

And I could absolutely murder a **piranha** sandwich!

Candelabra the Cat x

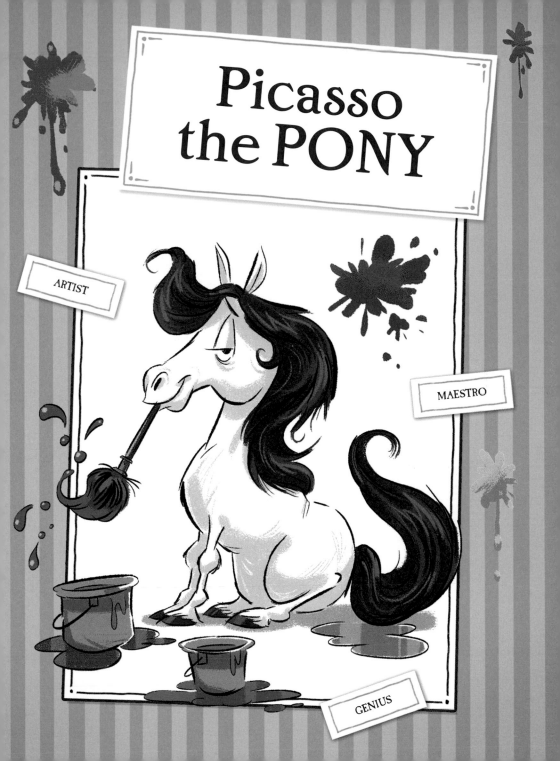

Picasso
the PONY

Molly Coddle was a girl who had been born with a silver spoon in her mouth. **Literally.** Her mother had accidentally swallowed the spoon when she was pregnant.

While in the womb, Baby Molly would kick her mother's tummy if she hadn't had enough food.

THUMP!

"OOF!"

And once, when her mother was shovelling down as much chocolate soufflé as fast as she could, the baby kicked so hard that she gulped down the spoon too.

THUMP!

GULP!

From the moment of her birth, baby Molly threw a tantrum if she didn't get what she wanted. Her wealthy parents indulged their daughter's every whim. Lord and Lady Coddle gave their baby:

GOLD-PLATED nappies

A **diamond-encrusted** dummy

A pair of **BRONZE** booties

A romper suit made from the **softest** cashmere

A pram designed and built by the **ROLLS-ROYCE** motorcar company

A solid **silver** bonnet

A handmade **mahogany** cot lined with only the finest *silks*

A **cut-glass** milk bottle

A solid **marble** teddy bear to cuddle at night

A one-hundred-piece *orchestra* on call day and night to play "Twinkle, Twinkle, Little Star" to send her off to sleep.

As she grew up, Molly's demands became more and more outlandish:

A **ROBOT** to do all her homework for her

A bath as big as a *swimming pool*

A private **ski slope**
on the roof

A dinner service made of the finest **Swiss chocolate**
so if she was still hungry after her meal she could
eat the plates and bowls too

A **solid-gold** pair of sunglasses (though
sadly she couldn't see through them)

A television the size of a football pitch

A football pitch the size of a **television** (less useful)

Rose petals thrown in her path
wherever she walked

A **JET PACK** to save
her having to walk
up stairs

Her own **Wendy house** in the garden that
was much bigger than the family home.

Now, I know what you are thinking: *this book is about the world's worst pets! NOT the world's worst children – GET ON WITH THE STORY!*

I am sorry.

AND STOP FILLING THE BOOK WITH LISTS JUST TO MAKE UP THE PAGE COUNT!

I said I am sorry.

STOP SAYING SORRY AND GET A MOVE ON!

Sorry.

YOU JUST SAID "SORRY" AGAIN! **SORRY!**

This story is about what happens when one of the world's worst pets meets one of the world's worst children.

Now, one day, Molly demanded a pony. Not just any pony.

"I want the *prettiest* pony in the world," bawled Molly, "as I am the *prettiest* girl in the world!"

So pony after pony was paraded in front of her, but she found fault with every single one of them.

"Too tall! Too short!

Too toothy! Not toothy enough!

Too fat! Too thin! Too dark! Too light!

Too horsey-looking!

Not horsey-looking enough!"

This went on for hours and hours.

Molly was **impossible!**

Lord and Lady Coddle were ready to give up when the final pony pranced into the garden. He was white in colour with a black mane, tail and hooves. His name was Picasso. Picasso the pony was a *pretty* little creature, but didn't he know it! He pointed his nose in the air, shook his mane and *flounced* up and down in front of Molly as if he were a fashion model on a Parisian catwalk.

PICASSO PARADED.

PICASSO POUTED.

PICASSO POSED.

PICASSO PRANCED.

PICASSO PREENED.

PICASSO PUCKERED.

PICASSO PIROUETTED.

PICASSO PIDDLED.

PICASSO SWISHED HIS TAIL AROUND AND AROUND, PERFORMING A LITTLE DANCE ROUTINE.

SWISH! SWOSH! SWUSH!

Finally, Picasso pulled a face that he believed was even more beautiful than his actual face, but was actually a bit WEIRD.

You can judge for yourself:

BEFORE

AFTER

"What about this one, my dearest Molly?" asked Lady Coddle. "His name is Picasso!"

"HMMM!" replied the **ghastly** girl, thinking out loud.

The pony snorted. *"SNORT!"* It was as if he were saying, "How could you turn ME down?"

"He's the very last pony in the country, my sweetest!"

said Lord Coddle. "If you don't like Picasso, then I'm sorry, my angel, but there is no pony."

"He's the wrong colour!" exclaimed Molly.

Picasso reared on to his hind legs and let out a deafening cry. **"NEIGH!"**

Lord and Lady Coddle shared a sorrowful look. They'd been in impossible places like this with their only child thousands of times before.

"Well, what colour would you like Picasso to be, my darling?" asked Father.

"White and black!" she shouted.

Picasso looked incensed. His eyes bulged and he bared his teeth.

"GRRRR!"

Molly's father studied the pony again. "He is white and black, my angel!"

"HE IS BLACK AND WHITE, YOU FOOL!" bawled Molly.

"NEIGH!" neighed the pony, thumping his head with his hoof.

THONK!

"Oh, so you would like Picasso to be black with a white

mane, tail and hooves, my fairy princess?"
asked Mother.

"YES! BUTLER!" called Molly.

The elderly butler, Hobble, shuffled over.

"Yes, my lady?"

"Go into town and fetch as many pots of black and
white paint as you can fit in the Rolls!"

"*NEIGH!*" neighed Picasso.

"Very good, miss!" replied the butler, shuffling off.

"AND FOR GOODNESS' SAKE, HOBBLE, HURRY!"

The ancient man tried his best to pick up his pace, but
it was like a sloth overtaking a snail. S. L. O. W.

However, Hobble drove like a demon!

ZOOM!

Well, it wasn't *his* Rolls he was thrashing!

In seconds, the butler was back at Coddle Court with a
car full of paint pots.

"You are not really going to paint the horse, are you?" asked Father.

"YES!" replied Molly.

"That's awfully cruel," said Mother.

"You are awfully cruel for buying me the wrong colour pony!"

"But it's **wrong** to paint any animal!" said Father.

"I don't care!" she bawled as she led her pet into the barn.

While Picasso bucked and kicked, Molly painted him black where he was white and white where he was black.

BEFORE

AFTER

"Right!" said Molly, leading Picasso out of the barn.

"Now, let's see how fast you can go, you great lump!"

She backed up, and then took a running jump, landing hard on the pony's back.

THUD!

"*NEIGH!*" he neighed as he galloped off across the lawn, leaping over hedges and heading for the fields.

"MAKE HIM STOP! MAKE HIM STOP!" yelled Molly.

She slapped Picasso's behind hard to bring him to a halt.

SLAP!

This had the opposite effect. The animal just galloped faster.

SWOOSH!

Picasso smiled a sinister smile. He was clearly relishing the chance to **frighten** this awful girl out of her wits!

"HELP!" yelled Molly.

SWOOOOOOSH!

Lord and Lady Coddle watched their daughter disappear off into the distance.

"Well, I suppose I should do something," remarked Father.

"No need to rush," said Mother. "Maybe we should have tea and scones first and enjoy the view."

"Hobble!" called out Father.

The elderly butler hobbled over.

"Yes, your lordship?"

"Tea and scones on the lawn, please."

"Very good, sir."

"And then afterwards, if you wouldn't mind awfully, please chase after the pony and bring our darling daughter home safely," said Lady Coddle.

"I will do my best, your ladyship."

It was midnight by the time Molly got home on a now puffed-out Picasso. Needless to say, the girl was in a

FOUL MOOD!

"I HATE PICASSO! IF HE'S NOT GONE BY THE MORNING, I WILL SCREAM AND SCREAM AND SCREAM UNTIL I AM SICK!"

Picasso looked smugger than ever. The pony would not have to stay with this **rotten** family another day. He sashayed back into the barn for the night. With a flick of his tail, he slammed the door behind him.

SLAP! SLAM!

Just before he was about to lie down on some hay and wait for dawn, Picasso spotted all the paints and brushes. The pony picked up a brush in his mouth. In moments, he had restored himself to his proper colouring. White with black bits not black with white bits.

On a roll, the pony decided to splash some paint on

the stable wall too. By dawn, Picasso had created an enormous painting of...

MOLLY CODDLE!

It showed the girl in all her *gruesome* glory, yelling her guts out.

"WAAAAH!"

Like the famous Spanish painter he was named after, Picasso stepped back to admire his work. He chuckled to himself.

"NEIGH! NEIGH! NEIGH!"

Picasso the painting pony had captured the monster to perfection.

*

Molly Coddle woke up at dawn in a **RAGE**.

"ARGH!"

She was still **fuming** over what had happened yesterday with Picasso!

In her nightdress, Molly stomped out of the house and across the lawn to the barn.

STOMP! STOMP! STOMP!

"I HOPE THAT CURSED CREATURE IS GONE OR THERE WILL BE TROUBLE!" she bellowed.

Hearing her, Mother and Father dashed out of the house. It was still early, and they hadn't arranged for Picasso to be collected yet.

Inside the barn, the girl snatched the paintbrush out of Picasso's mouth. "Bad pony! Look what a mess you have made of the wall! I hate you! I hate you! I HATE YOU!"

The pony reared up on to his hind legs. *"NEIGH!"*

When the lord and lady stumbled into the barn, they were shocked by what they saw.

There was Molly with a paintbrush in her hand, standing in front of the most extraordinary picture.

"My goodness me!"
exclaimed Mother. "That is stunning!"

"What?" demanded Molly.

"Our darling daughter is an **artistic genius!**"
added Father.

"A what what?" asked the girl.

"And we thought you were multi-talentless, Molly! How wrong we were!" said Mother.

"She has an incredible gift!" agreed Father.

"For what?" asked Molly, baffled.

"Painting! You did paint that wonderful self-portrait behind you, didn't you?"

Molly looked round at it. "Yep!" she lied.

"NEIGH!" protested Picasso, furiously shaking his head.

Mother and Father rushed over to embrace their daughter. "Such a remarkable painting from a girl of just ten. You will be famous all over the world," said Father.

"I will?" said Molly, her eyes lighting up with glee.

"And be rich! Rich! RICH! RICH!"

added Mother.

"Richer," corrected Molly.

"So, let's take Picasso away, and let you get on with your painting, Molly the **artistic genius!**" said Father as he started to lead the pony away.

"Well, let's not be too hasty!" said Molly. "I have

grown to rather like the little beast. Haven't I?" She leaned in to give the pony a hug.

"*NEIGH!*" went Picasso, baring his teeth menacingly.

"Do as I say, or I'll have you melted down and turned into glue!" she hissed.

Picasso forced a smile.

"Well, it's one thing painting on the wall, but another thing showing your art in a gallery," said Father. "We will send Hobble into town to buy a hundred canvases!"

In no time, the canvases arrived, and the barn was set up as Molly Coddle's **art studio.**

"We would love to watch you paint!" said Mother.

"Rather!" agreed Father.

"No! No! No!" snapped Molly. "I can only work when no one is watching me! Well, no one except Picasso. Now out! Shoo! Shoo! Shoo!"

With that, she shoved her parents out of the barn and set to work.

"Now, Picasso, paint!" she ordered, shoving the brush into the pony's mouth. "Paint me a hundred pictures, or you will find yourself in a tube of superglue!"

Picasso had no choice. By dusk, he had painted a hundred pictures of Molly. Each one captured her *ghastliness* to greater and greater perfection.

Molly Coddle snatched the brush out of Picasso's mouth and signed her name on the bottom of each and every canvas.

SCRIBBLE! SCRIBBLE! SCRIBBLE!

WORK BY THE ARTISTIC GENIUS
MOLLY CODDLE.

Next, Molly shouted out of the barn door, "FINISHED!"
Instantly, her parents galloped into the barn.

"Superb!" "TREMENDOUS!"

"Striking!" "DAZZLING!"

"Spectacular!" "Marvellous!"

"Inspired!" "Outstanding!"

"Stunning!" "Astounding!"

The words of praise just kept tumbling out of the pair.

"I will call the art gallery at once!" said Father.

"Our little girl is one of the greatest painters of
all time!" added Mother.

"NEIGH!" protested Picasso, shaking his head wildly.

Molly hissed in the pony's ear. "You play along with
this, or SQUIRT!"

The girl mimed squeezing glue out of a tube!

*

Within days, Molly Coddle had her first exhibition at a huge gallery. The world sat up and took notice of this ten-year-old girl who had painted herself with remarkable **accuracy!**

All one hundred paintings sold for **millions!**

Molly Coddle became filthy richer and *disgustingly* famous.

She was on TV! On the cover of every magazine! There was even a film of her life called MOLLY: THE GREATEST GIRL WHO EVER LIVED! Molly came up with the title.

But Molly, being Molly, wanted MORE! MORE! MORE!

So poor Picasso was forced to paint more and more and more pictures!

The canvases became bigger, and now instead of pots of paint there were **vats.**

The new exhibition of paintings sold for billions!

The next canvases were the size of a house, so a tall platform had to be erected from which to paint.

To fill the canvases, the paint was kept below in a series of paddling pools that covered the floor of the barn.

One night, Picasso had been up on the platform with Molly since dawn. He had already painted fifty canvases that day, but still the girl demanded more.

"ANOTHER, PICASSO! ANOTHER!"

The pony had had enough. He loathed this *awful* child and refused to do another thing for her. In protest, he spat the paintbrush out of his mouth.

SPLUT!

It hit the girl on the head…

BOINK!

…and fell to the floor.

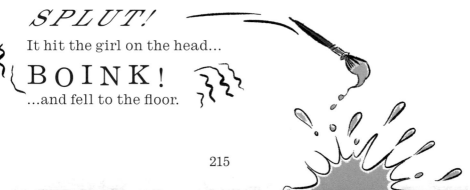

215

THUNK!

"PICK THAT UP!" screeched Molly.

"NEIGH!" replied Picasso.

"Don't you 'neigh' me, Picasso! If you don't pick that up right now, I will scream and scream and scream until I am sick!"

"NEIGH!"

"Pick it up! Or I will boot you on the bottom!"

Picasso shook his head. His eyes bulged and his ears flapped in anger. "NEIGH!"

"Right! You asked for it!" began Molly, swinging her leg to gain some momentum. "Three! Two! One!"

Just as her boot was about to make contact with Picasso's bottom, the pony lurched into her.

BUMP!

Picasso pushed the girl backwards.

"ARGH!"

Now she was toppling off the platform, flapping her arms around as if attempting to fly.

"NOOOO!" she cried as she grabbed hold of the pony's tail to stop herself from falling.

Picasso smiled to himself. He was going to enjoy this.

The pony began swirling his tail **round** and **round**.

WHIRR!

Molly Coddle held on as if her life depended on it, which it did. Soon she was nothing but a *BLUR!*

Then the pony flicked his tail. Molly lost her grip and was sent flying up in the air.

"ARGH!"

WHIZZ!

As the law of gravity states, what goes **up**, must come **down**.

"NOOOOOOOOO!" she cried as she sailed down into the pool of blue paint below.

SPLOOSH!

At last, Picasso had got his **REVENGE!**

"NEIGH!" he cried out as he reared up on his hind legs in celebration. However, up on that tall platform, he lost his balance too. The pony toppled backwards!

WHOOSH!

Picasso plummeted into a pool of purple paint!

The pools were deep, so it was hard to climb out. Picasso just managed to scramble over the side to safety. As he stood there, Molly grabbed hold of his tail and yanked herself out. The girl landed on her pony's back.

SPLUT!

The paint was drying fast and within moments the pair found themselves not just stuck to each other but stuck still. Trapped together looking like a statue.

At dusk, Lord and Lady Coddle marched into the barn.

"Molly!" called Father.

"Where are you, dearest?" asked Mother.

Molly was stuck still with paint, so couldn't make a sound.

"She must have gone!" said Father, searching the barn.

"Picasso has gone too!" remarked Mother.

"But behold this beautiful statue! Their parting gift to the world!"

So Molly Coddle was put in pride of place in the greatest gallery in the world. A fitting tribute to a great artist – con artist, that is. Painted blue, she looked like a giant Smurf.

Molly was sitting on top of purple Picasso, who looked like a life-sized My Little Pony.

The world's worst pet and the world's worst child. They **hated** each other. Their punishment was to be **stuck** together.

Forever.

Silly Sid's
SNAKE

Snakes slither to the top on a list of the
world's worst pets. They are joint world's worst
with spiders (**creepy** AND crawly), bats
(all that **blood-sucking**
nonsense), sharks (like to

eat children), hippopotamuses (take up
too much space) and worms (not much
conversation).

So, what would happen if one of
your parents brought home a snake?

That is what Silly Sid did.

"Kids! Look what I bought you down the pub!"
announced Silly Sid as he burst through the door of
the family home. Silly Sid was wearing
his usual mismatched
colours and
patterns.

As always, it looked as if he'd got dressed in the dark. His hair was a wild bush, his glasses were on all wonky and he had his right shoe on his left foot and his left shoe on his right. Well, Silly Sid was rather silly, as his name suggests. Over his shoulder, he was carrying a large cloth sack. Something was wriggling and wraggling* and wruggling** around inside it.

WRIGGLE! WRAGGLE! WRUGGLE!

Can you guess what it is? You can? Oh yes, the title of this story does give it away a bit. DRAT! DOUBLE DRAT! And TRIPLE DRAT!

Well, let's not spoil the surprise for his poor children just yet!

Silly Sid's three not-at-all-silly kids stopped playing Snakes and Ladders, and rushed over excitedly to greet him. Like most children, they had wanted a pet for as long as they could remember.

"Is it a kitten?"

"Is it a hamster?"

"Is it a bunny?"

"WHOA! WHOA! WHOA!" exclaimed their dad.

"Just wait and see!"

* Wraggling means wruggling.
** Wruggling means wraggling. See your Walliamsictionary.

With that, he reached into his bag and pulled out a... **SNAKE!** *"HISS!"*

Not just any snake – one of the **biggest** species of snake in the world... A PYTHON! The snake stuck out its tongue, then, with what looked like a smile, wrapped itself round Silly Sid... and began to *squeeze!*

SQUOOSH!

"HISS!" hissed the snake, its eyes bulging with delight. This was one scary snake!

Silly Sid just smiled his silly smile.

"ARGH!"

"HELP!"

"GET IT AWAY FROM US!" screamed the children.

"What's all this noise?" cried Mum

as she stormed into the living room with her hair in curlers.

Mum's name was Nancy. Nancy had been married to Silly Sid for twenty long, silly years. She thought she'd seen it all before, but this time Silly Sid had done something sillier than ever!

"Oh no, Silly Sid, what on earth have you done now?" cried Nancy on seeing the snake.

Immediately, she tried to yank the python off her husband. Any moment now, it was going to squeeze the life out of him.

"HISS!"

"What do you mean?" he asked innocently as the snake wrapped itself round his neck. Silly Sid didn't know he was silly, which added an extra layer of silliness.

Silly Sid's life had been one long list of silly mistakes:

SILLY SID'S SLIP-UPS!

There was the time Nancy sent Silly Sid out to buy a pint of milk and he came back with a caravan.

Or there was the famous incident when Silly Sid walked out of the door with a flowerpot on his head rather than his hat.

Or when Silly Sid sat and watched the microwave oven for an hour, thinking it was the television.

Or the time he put his *flip-flops* in the toaster instead of slices of bread.

Or that time he filled the paddling pool with **jelly** instead of water.

Or when he fell asleep in his cupboard, thinking it was his bed.

Or, worst of all, the time Silly Sid mistook his wife for a garden **gnome**. He brought the gnome on holiday with him, leaving Nancy at home.

However, of all Silly Sid's mistakes, bringing home a python was by far the silliest.

"The kids wanted a pet!" protested Silly Sid.

"Not one like that, you silly, silly man!" snapped Nancy as she just managed to pull the python off him.

"HISS!"

The huge snake slithered along the floor, and the kids leaped behind the sofa.

"HISS!"

All three children were called Bob. Bob, Bob and not forgetting Bob. Silly Sid named all his children Bob so that he wouldn't forget what they were called. Even though one of them was a girl. He tried to call his wife Bob too, but Nancy was having none of it!

"NOOO!" screamed Bob.

"PLEASE!" yelled the other Bob.

Bob

Bob

Bob

"I AM S-S-S-SCARED!" cried out the girl Bob.

Nancy yelled at her husband, "Silly Sid! The Bobs wanted something cute and cuddly, like a puppy!"

"This is a puppy!" stated Silly Sid with a smile.

The man wasn't joking.

Silly Sid really was that silly.

"You what?" said everyone else (except the snake, who may well have been thinking it).

The snake slithered up on to a shelf, knocking off all the books with one swish of its long, thick tail.

DONK!   **DONK!**   **DONK!**

"That is NOT a puppy, you silly, silly, silly man!" shouted Nancy.

"The bloke in the pub, Mr Shifty, who flogged it to me, swore it was!" replied Silly Sid.

"Well, that Mr Shifty saw you coming! You seriously believed him?"

The snake was now dangling upside down from the lightshade.

"*HISS!*" it hissed, as it swung from side to side in obvious delight at its new playground. This was so much better than being in a sack!

"Yeah! And it was a bargain. 'Last puppy in the litter,' he said. Only a hundred quid."

"A HUNDRED QUID!" exclaimed Nancy. "I GIVE UP!"

"I'm not stupid. I asked Mr Shifty why the puppy was so big. And he told me it was a fully grown puppy."

"Dad! A fully grown puppy would be a dog," chipped in one of the Bobs.

"DAD! He can't be a puppy! He's got no fur!" said another Bob.

"That's how puppies are born, Bobs!" replied their father. "Without any fur! Mr Shifty said!"

The snake slithered on to Nancy's shoulder and began wrapping itself round her!

"*HISS!*" hissed the snake, its eyes glowing with glee at the **TERROR** it was causing.

"C-C-CRIPES!" cried Nancy, her teeth chattering with fear. "G-G-GET THIS THING OFF M-M-ME!"

The three Bobs leaped over the sofa to help their mother. Together, they heaved on the snake's tail. But the snake was so big and powerful that it lifted the children high into the air!

WHOOSH!

"ARGH!" they cried.

"It can't be a puppy, Dad. Look!
It's got **no legs!**" said a Bob.

"Puppies' legs grow when they get older!"
replied Silly Sid.

"*HISS!*" hissed the snake again, its long forked
tongue licking Nancy's nose.

"If it's a puppy, then why does it keep *hissing?*"
asked another Bob.

"He's only little. He hasn't learned to bark yet!"
reasoned Silly Sid. "Come on, Fido. Give us a bark!"

"*HISS!*" hissed the snake, looking mightily
confused.

"NEARLY!" exclaimed Silly Sid.

"You called him Fido?" exclaimed Nancy. She couldn't believe her ears!

"Fido is a perfect name for a puppy!"

"For the last time, Fido is NOT A PUPPY!" she said. "Now, Silly Sid, for goodness' sake, help the children down. Then get this thing off me!"

One by one, Silly Sid plucked his Bobs off the snake as if they were apples from a tree. He set them down safely on the floor. Then he yanked hard on his pet's tail.

TUG!

"*HISS!*" hissed the snake angrily as he unravelled at speed.

Poor Nancy was sent spinning.

WHIRR!

"Come on, Fido," said Silly Sid, oblivious to the mayhem he'd just caused. "There's a good boy! Let's go for a nice walk!"

Then he put a dog collar round his pet's neck (hard to know where that is on a snake, as it all looks like neck), before attaching a lead. "Bob, Bob, Bob and Nancy! Me and Fido are off to the park! BYE!"

"*HISS!*" hissed the snake in fury as he was dragged along the floor.

Nancy was still spinning as they left the room.

WHIRR!   "H-H-H-E-E-E-L-L-L-P-P-P!"

Taking his snake for a walk around the park was just one of the silly things Sid did with his new pet.

One Sunday afternoon, Silly Sid brought Fido to an old folks' home to visit his elderly mother. He thought the old people would love stroking the puppy.

"HISS!"

Oh my word! You've never seen old folk move so fast!

There were sparks coming off the Zimmer frames!

SIZZLE!

It is important to make sure your pet's teeth are clean, so Silly Sid brought Fido to the vet. However, when the vet tried to clean the snake's teeth, she very

nearly lost an arm.

"HISS!"

CHOMP!

"HELP!"

At the end of every day, Silly Sid would give his pet a bath.

"There's a good boy! Let's get you nice and clean!" he would say.

SPLISH! SPLASH! SPLOSH!

Pythons like being underwater, so it was always a struggle to get Fido out of the bath.

Every time Silly Sid tried, the snake would wrap himself round his master's arm and drag him in.

"AH!" SPLOOSH!

"HISS! HISS! HISS!"

Fido grew and grew until he was longer than a bus. One morning, Silly Sid shocked his wife and the Bobs with his silliest idea yet. He gathered them all in the living room to announce his news. Meanwhile, Fido caused more mayhem. The snake slithered along the windowsill, knocking all the flowerpots off with a swish of his tail.

"HISS!"

SWISH! *SWISH!* *SWISH!*

They landed on all the Bobs' heads.

BOOM! BANG! BOOF!

"OOF!"

"OUCH!"

"ORRF!"

"Hush, please!" began Silly Sid. "Thank you, Bobs. Now, as Fido has been such a good puppy—"

At that moment, the snake knocked a huge porcelain clown off the shelf. It landed on Nancy's head.

SWISH!

"HISS!"

DOINK!

SMASH!

"YOUCH!" she shrieked.

"I did ask for hush, Nancy!" chided Silly Sid. "Thank you! Now, as Fido has been such a good puppy, I have decided to enter him for the greatest dog show on earth. **RUFFS!**"

Silly Sid's family burst out laughing.

"HA! HA! HA!"

"I have never heard anything so funny in my life!"

"That is hilarious!"

"I laughed so much that some *pee-pee* dribbled out!" said one of the boy Bobs.

Fido stared at them, not liking the loud noise at all.

"*HISS!*" he hissed, sticking out his forked tongue in displeasure.

Nancy was absolutely tickled pink. "Oh! Silly Sid, you have out-sillied yourself this time! That is the silliest thing I have ever heard!"

"Why?" asked Silly Sid. Because he was so silly, he failed to see the funny side.

"BECAUSE FIDO'S A SNAKE!" his family chimed in together. "HA! HA! HA!"

"STOP BEING SO SILLY!" exclaimed Silly Sid. "Fido will win **RUFFS** and I will prove you all wrong!"

They all burst out laughing again. "HA! HA! HA!" They had never laughed so **loud** or so long in all their lives!

"We'll be watching you both on TV!" chuckled Nancy.

So Silly Sid had set himself an impossible task. How on earth could a snake win a dog show?

As it turned out, with ease!

Please let me explain...

Ruffs

RUFFS is like a beauty pageant for dogs. Only the most well-behaved and perfectly groomed dog is awarded the title **BEST IN SHOW.** Thousands of dogs from around the world take part, and it is beamed into living rooms everywhere through the magic of television.

So Silly Sid put Fido back on the lead, which the snake loathed...

"HISS!"

...and took him off to the huge hall where **RUFFS** was taking place.

The place was teaming with dogs, dogs and more dogs.

Their owners were there too, but the dogs were the **STARS.**

These were the most pampered pooches in the world.

Amongst them were the dog superstars:

Mimi the **Maltese,** who was handing out paw prints to her adoring fans...

Abdul the **Afghan hound,** who was giving workshops on how best to blow-dry your hair... and, last but not least, there was **Polina** the ***Pomeranian.***

Her fur was as white as snow, her ears were perfectly pointed up like little pink bows on top of her head and she had the *fluffiest* tail. No wonder Polina won **RUFFS** year after year. The Pomeranian was selling selfies with her for a thousand pounds a pop. If you didn't pay up fast enough in cash, Polina would bite you on the bottom. This was one wicked little dog.

CHOMP!

"YEOW!"

So, into this cathedral of canines came a big scary snake.

As soon as Silly Sid brought Fido into the hall, there was chaos! It was

POOCH PANDEMONIUM!

"WOOF! WOOF! WOOF!"

The dogs went barking mad. They went to flee. The owners didn't stand a chance. Their dogs yanked so hard on their leads that their owners were pulled to the ground.

DOOF!

Then they were dragged on their bellies down through the hall, into the streets and all the way home!

"STOP!"

241

Only one dog remained. The littlest, **yappiest,** fiercest dog: Polina.

"YAP! YAP! YAP!"

Fido slithered over to her, dragging Silly Sid all the way.

SLITHER! SLITHER! SLITHER!

"WHOA THERE, BOY!"

"HISS!" hissed Fido at the little dog. The snake was used to frightening those around him, but Polina was one brave pooch. She just kept yapping.

"YAP! YAP! YAP!"

"HISS!" hissed Fido again. His eyes bulged and his mouth opened, and for a moment it looked as if the dog might end up as a snake snack.

"HISS!" The snake licked his lips.

"Come away now, Fido," ordered Silly Sid, tugging on the lead. Then, just as the snake was distracted for a moment by his master, Polina went on the attack!

"YAP! YAP! YAP!"

A bottom-biting expert, she raced round to the back of the snake. Struggling to find the snake's actual bottom, she bit hard on to the end of Fido's tail instead.

CHOMP!

So hard that the snake shot up into the air...

WHOOSH!

...and let out a hiss of pain!

"HHHIIISSSSS!"

Fido bit on to a **RUFFS** sign that was hanging from the ceiling! Poor Silly Sid was dangling below, still holding tight to his pet's lead.

"HELP!" cried Silly Sid.

Polina took a running jump and leaped into the air.

She bit Silly Sid on the bottom. Not once, but twice!

CHOMP! CHOMP!

Once for each buttock.

"YEOW!" howled Silly Sid in pain.

This made Fido furious. Still holding on to the sign, the snake swung his tail down to the ground and hooked the little dog.

"**YAP! YAP! YAP!**" yapped Polina as she was lifted high into the air.

WHOOSH!

To get his revenge, Fido began spinning the little dog round and round.

"LET GO, FIDO! THERE'S A GOOD DOG!" ordered Silly Sid.

"**YAP! YAP! YAP!**"

The faithful pet did just that. He let go of Polina mid spin and let her zoom through the air.

WHIZZ!

"**YAP! YAP! YAP!**"

Polina crashed through the roof.

SMASH!

244

She rocketed through the sky.

WHOOSH!

The Pomeranian was travelling so fast she landed in

Pomerania!

DOOF!

"YAP!"

With no dogs left in the hall, the **RUFFS** judges had to name a winner. Fearing they were going to have the life squeezed out of them if they didn't let the python win, Fido was named **BEST IN SHOW!**

"HISS!" hissed the snake in celebration, performing a little victory dance by bouncing around on his tail.

BOING! BOING! BOING!

"YES!" exclaimed Silly Sid, who for once in his life had achieved something that was definitely **not** silly. He wrapped his arms round Fido, and together they twirled across the hall as if they were ballroom dancers!

SWISH!

Nancy and the Bobs watched the whole thing open-mouthed in shock from home as it unfolded live on TV.

When the **triumphant** pair finally returned home, it was Silly Sid's and Fido's turn to laugh.

"HA! HA! HA!"

"HISS! HISS! HISS!"

"Now that Fido has won the biggest dog show in the world," began Silly Sid, "will you accept that he really is a dog?"

Nancy and the three Bobs looked at each before replying, "NOOOOOOOOO!"

"You lot are sooooo silly!" said Silly Sid. He turned to Fido, who nodded his head in agreement.

"HISS!"

The Great GRIZZLY BEAR Mystery

WHAT SPECIES OF ANIMAL do you think would make the world's **very** worst pet?

This is the story of two children who were determined to bring one of the most **terrifying** animals on earth into their home.

A GRIZZLY BEAR.

What happened next may **surprise** you.

Let me begin this tale by introducing you to the two children. They were twins: a girl and a boy named Lois and Mylo. They lived with their two fathers in a windmill at the top of a hill. From there they had a view of a **deep, dark forest** below.

Now, the children always whined and whined and whined about **not** having a pet.

All the other children in their local village had them. There were dogs, cats, rabbits, ferrets and mice. One child even had a **hawk!** So Lois and Mylo pleaded and pleaded with their fathers. One they called Daddy, and the other they called Papa.

"Why can't we have a pet, Daddy?" begged Lois.

"It's not fair!" added Mylo.

It was the first thing they spoke about when they woke up in the morning and the last thing when they went to bed at night. All day, every day, they went on and on and ON about having a pet.

In the end, their fathers were driven bananas. So, one evening when the children had been pleading nonstop for several hours, they finally caved in.

"ALL RIGHT! ALL RIGHT!" snapped Daddy.

"YOU CAN HAVE A PET!" added Papa.

"YES!" cried the twins, hugging each other. They fell silent for a moment.

"Peace at last!" exclaimed Daddy.

"But which pet shall we get?" asked Lois excitedly.

"OH! Any animal you like!" replied Daddy.

"Just no more going on about it!" added Papa.

This proved to be a huge mistake. And I mean HUGE! The twins looked at each other in disbelief.

"Any animal we like, Daddy?" asked Lois.

"Any one!" he replied.

"Promise, Papa?" said Mylo.

"WE PROMISE!" declared Papa.

"YES!" exclaimed the twins.

Then they tumbled up the long, winding staircase to their bedroom at the very top of the windmill.

As they could have any pet they chose, it seemed silly to pick an animal so many other children had, like a dog or a cat or a mouse. So together they sat on the rug and searched for inspiration in their favourite book, **The BIG book of BLOODCURDLING BEASTS.** Like many children, the twins were far more interested in the **scary** animals than the nice ones.

"The killer whale is one of the **deadliest** creatures on Earth!" read Lois.

"Well, let's get one of those, then!" exclaimed Mylo.

"Where are we going to keep it?"

"In the bath, of course!"

"What about bath time? I am **not** sharing a bath with a **great big whale!**" said the girl.

That was the end of that.

No killer whale.

"LOOK!" exclaimed Mylo.

"It says here that **hippopotamuses** kill more people every year than sharks!"

"Wow! Let's get one, then! But, hang on, who would pick up the hippo dung?" asked Lois.

That was the end of that.

No hippopotamus.

"I know! I know! I know!" cried Lois, snatching the book back. "We should get a **crocodile!**"

"Who would clean its teeth?" asked Mylo.

That was the end of that.

No crocodile.

The twins were running out of ideas when they turned to the final page in

The **BIG** book of **BLOODCURDLING BEASTS**, only to see a picture of a gruesome grizzly bear.

"I've got it, Mylo!" cooed Lois. "LOOK!"

Mylo studied the picture. He was more than a little alarmed by the creature's:

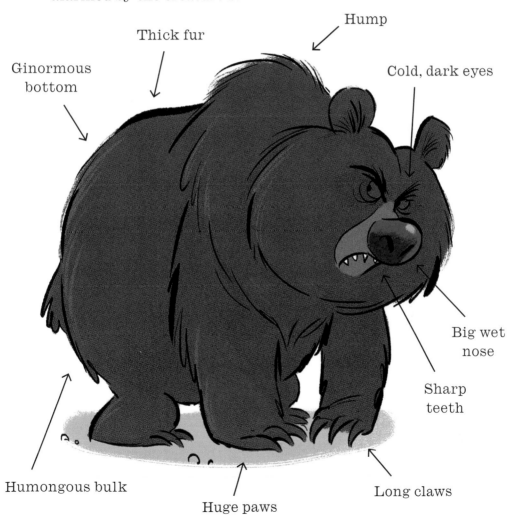

Hump

Thick fur

Ginormous
bottom

Cold, dark eyes

Big wet
nose

Sharp
teeth

Humongous bulk

Huge paws

Long claws

"Aren't **grizzly bears** just a teeny bit too **bloodcurdling**, even for us?" he asked.

"Nonsense! It would be just like having a real-life teddy bear."

"That is huge!"

"EXACTLY!"

"And eats people."

"Nobody's perfect!" Lois replied, snapping the book shut. "That's settled, then! We are getting our very own **grizzly bear** as a pet!"

Mylo smiled weakly, not wanting to look like a scaredy-cat in front of his sister.

Now, how would they find a **grizzly bear?**

There was a legend about one living in the forest, though no one had ever seen it. There must be some place one could buy a **grizzly bear.** But where?

Neither child had a clue, so they rushed to their fathers to ask them.

"You want a what?" spluttered Daddy.

"A bear!" said Lois.

"A teddy bear?" asked Papa.

"No. A real-life **grizzly bear!**"

At once, both men spat out their coffee.

SPLURGE!

"You can't have a real-life **grizzly bear** as a pet!" said Daddy.

"Why not?" demanded Lois.

"Because a **grizzly bear** is a wild animal – not a pet!" replied Papa.

"It would be the WORLD'S WORST PET!" added Daddy. "It would eat us out of house and home!"

"And then it would eat US too!" agreed Papa.

Lois elbowed her brother to prompt him.

"But you promised us we could have any pet we wanted!" said Mylo.

"Yes, not for a million billion trillion years did I think you were going to choose a **grizzly bear!**" spluttered Daddy.

"NOT FAIR!" said Lois, stamping her foot so hard that a picture fell off the wall. **DOINK!**

"All right! All right! We'll think of something – won't we, Papa?" said Daddy.

"Will we, Daddy?" asked Papa, not the least bit convinced.

"Run off up to bed, you two, and we can make a plan in the morning!"

If the fathers thought their children would forget about their promise in the morning, they couldn't have been more wrong. At dawn, the twins raced into their parents' bedroom and jumped up and down on their bed demanding…

"BEAR! BEAR! BEAR!"

"All right! All right!" said Papa.

"Calm down!" added Daddy, before sneezing at all the feathers from the pillow floating up into the air.

"ATISHOO! Now, me and Papa have had a talk, and later today we're going to take you both to a very special pet shop…"

"YES!" cried the kids.

"And if they happen to have a **grizzly bear** then maybe, just maybe, we can get one!"

"YES!"

The children busied themselves up in their bedroom, pretending to be dinosaurs having a battle.

"GRRR!"

"ROAR!"

Hours went by until Daddy called up to them, "IT'S TIME TO GO!"

They cycled on the family's four-seater bicycle (or quadricycle) to the pet shop.

It was a strange little place at the far end of their local village that the children had never seen before. A sign over the front read:

Daddy gave them some money, and said, "You go in. We need to pop off now, but Papa will be here when you come out of the shop to cycle home with you!"

The twins thought this was odd, but pushed open the shop door.

CREAK!

"Welcome to " said a tall man with a big bushy beard, who appeared from behind the counter. He was a shifty-looking fellow, with dark glasses, a pork-pie hat and a crumpled brown overall. "I am Pete. Now come in and shut that door behind you."

The twins shared a look but did what they were told.

Pete pulled down his dark glasses a little bit to get a better look at the pair. "You are real children, aren't you?"

Mylo and Lois were baffled.

"Yes, of course we are real children," Lois replied.

"Just checking," said Pete. "We don't want any undercover police in here, now, do we?"

Neither twin was sure what to say.

"Why would police be in a pet shop?" asked Lois.

"Well," he began, glancing out of the grimy little window in case there was anyone outside. "You see, at PETE'S PETS we don't have your everyday animals – your hamsters, your gerbils, your goldfish – see? Oh no. They are all rather small and boring. We have your, shall we say, bigger pets? The bigger the better."

"Well, that's what we wanted," replied Mylo, gaining confidence.

"PERFECTO! You have come to the right place. So, what can I do for you?"

Pete climbed on a ladder that *whizzed* around the floor on wheels. Behind the counter there were wooden

its big furry behind out
and made a rude noise
in their direction.

PFFT!

"I think that
gorilla just did a
bottom burp!" whispered Mylo.

"I'm glad we didn't choose
one!" replied Lois.

"Or a snake!"
suggested Pete.

The pet-shop owner flung
open another door. A **huge**
snake stretched its long neck
out. It looked **straight** at
the twins.

"HSSSSSSSSSS!"

doors, like a giant advent calendar. As he spoke, he flung open a door to reveal a pet.

"An elephant perhaps?" suggested Pete.

To the twins' amazement, a long trunk snaked out of the open door. It began patting the children on their heads.

THONK! THONK! THONK!

The children looked at each other in fear.

"Or a gorilla?" suggested Pete, flinging open the next door. The gorilla must have been in a mischievous mood as it waggled

"I'm sorry, Mr Pete, but these animals are just not **scary** enough!" began Lois. "Have you got any bears?"

"Bears?" spluttered Pete.

"Grizzly bears!" said Mylo.

"If you are sure…"

"**Yes!** We are sure!" replied Lois. She elbowed her brother.

"Oh yes!" he agreed. "Quite sure!"

"All right! Let's see if I have a **grizzly bear** back here somewhere!"

The pet-shop owner opened another door, and out popped the **huge** head of a terrifying **grizzly bear.**

"GRRRR!" it growled. It growled so loudly that the whole of **PETE'S PETS** began to shake.

{ R A T T L E ! ?}

Lois hid behind Mylo, and then Mylo hid behind Lois. Then they hid behind each other until they were nothing but a *blur.*

262

"You did say you wanted a **grizzly bear,** didn't you, kiddies?" asked Pete.

"Yes! But..." began Mylo.

"But...?"

"We said we were having a **grizzly bear** as a pet, and that's that!" said Lois, now hiding behind Mylo again.

"If you are sure?" asked Pete.

"We are sure, aren't we, Mylo?" asked Lois.

"GRRRR!" growled the bear again.

Once again the whole shop quaked.

RATTLE!

Mylo shook his head.

"See! My brother agrees!" exclaimed Lois.

"All right, then! Out you come!" called Pete. He opened the door behind him and out wobbled the most gigantic grizzly bear in the world.

"GRRR!" it growled again as it stumbled towards them on its back legs.

The twins stood on the spot, frozen with fear, as the bear gave them both a big bear hug.

The bear hugged them so tightly that it felt as if all the air were being squeezed out of them.

"Does it have a name?" squeaked Lois, her head nuzzled into the animal's thick brown fur.

"Griselda!" replied Pete. "Griselda the grizzly bear."

"How much is it?" asked Lois, her eyes nearly popping out at being squeezed so tightly.

Pete looked at the money in the girl's hand.

"That much!" he said, taking it. "Right, your papa will be here in just a moment!"

"How do you know that?" demanded Lois.

"Well, erm, um," spluttered the man. "I heard your daddy say that outside when he dropped you off."

"Oh," said Lois, not believing him entirely.

Pete the pet-shop man hurried back to his counter as the grizzly bear took the children's hands in its giant paws and led them out of the shop.

In moments, Papa appeared from round the back of PETE'S PETS , looking a little breathless.

"So, you two really got a grizzly bear!" he said in shock.

264

"GRRR!" growled the bear.

"Y-y-yes!" replied the twins.

"And you are sure you want to take your new pet home?"

The children looked at each other and replied, **"YES!"** though the look of alarm in their eyes told a different story.

"Come on, then! Let's all hop on!"

The four climbed on the quadricycle. Papa sat at the front, steering, then Mylo, then Lois and the bear at the very back. Griselda was surprisingly good at cycling. They looked quite a sight as they travelled through the village.

The villagers all stopped and stared at this strange foursome.

"The best thing to do," began Papa as he pedalled, "is pretend there is absolutely nothing strange about having a grizzly bear on the back of your quadricycle!"

With that, he waved at the vicar and called out, "Lovely morning, Vicar!"

The old lady was so shocked to see the bear that she crashed her trike and went straight through a hedge. **RUSTLE!**

The baker dropped a huge tiered wedding cake he was holding on the road.

SPLAT!

And the police officer was so amazed that he toppled backwards into the village pond.

SPLOSH!

They cycled along the path through the forest. There was the sound of rustling in the trees as they passed the deepest, darkest spot.

RUSTLE!

There was the sound of a growl echoing through the tall trees.

"G-G-G-R-R-R!"

Without a word, the four picked up the pace and cycled away.

WHIZZ!

They reached the windmill at the top of the hill not a moment too soon.

"Well, Griselda," said Lois, "this is your new home!"

"GRRR!" growled Griselda.

Lois went to lead her new pet inside the windmill, but Griselda had other ideas. The bear leaped on to one of the sails as it circled.

WHOOSH!

"GRRRR!" Griselda growled in glee, whirling through the air.

"NOOO, GRISELDA!" screamed Mylo.

"GET DOWN!" cried Lois.

Still, the bear went round and round and round.

WHIRR!

"I did warn you that a **grizzly bear** is not a pet. It's a wild animal!" said Papa. "It's not going to do what you ask!"

"So, what do we do?" pleaded Mylo.

"Bears like honey! Maybe we can tempt Griselda down with some!"

No sooner had Papa said this than Mylo dashed into the

windmill and returned with a gigantic jar of honey.

"GRISELDA! HONEY!" he called up.

At once, the bear leaped down to the ground with a

giant **THUD.**

"GRRRR!"

Griselda snatched the honey from Mylo with its huge

paws, then began pouring it down its throat.

GLUG! GLUG! GLUG!

It then tossed the

half-eaten jar aside.

HURL!

It rolled down the hill...

TRUNDLE!

...honey oozing out all the way.

OOZE!

Griselda then looked as if it were about to sneeze.

"AH! AH! AH...!" it went, before spraying the three

with snot. "TISHOOO!"

SPLAT!

The twins looked at each other in shock. They had only

had their pet for five minutes and they were already

drenched in bear snozzle.

This was only the beginning!

Once inside the windmill, the **grizzly bear** began to cause even more chaos.

Griselda licked their bedroom window with its long slobbery tongue, covering it in bear dribble…

SLURP!

"YUCK!"

Tucked itself into a ball and rolled towards the twins…

TRUNDLE!

…knocking them over like bowling pins.

BASH! BOSH!

"OUCH!"

"OUCH!"

Juggled the twins' pots of paint with its huge paws...

DONK! DONK! DONK!

...splashing their walls with it...

SPLOOSH!

"HELP!"

Ripped a huge hole in Mylo's undercrackers that were hanging up to dry.

RIP!

"NOOO!"

Tore out all the pages of

The **BIG** book of **BLOODCURDLING BEASTS**

and used them as toilet paper.

RIP! WIPE!

"PLEASE!"

Slid down the winding stair rail on its bottom at terrific speed.

WHIZZ!

"GRRR!"

"GRISELDAAA!"

Bounced up and down on the top bunk of their bunk beds until it snapped.

BOING! BOING! BOING!

SNUP! "STOP!"

Devoured every single chocolate biscuit in their tin...

CRUNCH! CRUNCH! CRUNCH!

...then ate the tin.

CLANK!

"PLEASE!"

Performed a daring dive off the toilet into the bath.

SPLOOOSH!

"GRISELDA!"

Dried itself by rubbing its wet, furry bottom on the bathroom mirror.

SQUEAK!

"EURGH!"

All throughout this dire display, the twins were looking to their father to make it STOP! But Papa just watched on with a wry smile at the bedlam the bear was creating.

Things took a turn for the very worst when Griselda decided to take a running jump on to the sofa, sending the twins flying high into the air!

DOOF!

WHOOSH!

"Y-Y-YIKES!"

They landed on the floor on their bottoms with a

THUD!

Mylo crawled over to his father. "Papa, please!" he pleaded. "Make it STOP!"

Papa looked over to his daughter. "What do you think, Lois?"

"I can't think any more. MY HEAD HURTS!"

"So shall we take Griselda back to PETE'S PETS and see if we can get a refund?"

"YES!" shouted the twins.

"Well, I think we should keep it," he said, looking over to the creature lying on the sofa.

"WHAT?" the children demanded, incredulous!

"Because it isn't really Griselda the **grizzly bear,** is it?"

The bear shook its head, before removing it.

IT WAS DADDY!

"DADDY!" cried the twins.

"I have been under here all along!" said Daddy. He and Papa hugged and kissed. The game was over!

"BUT WHY?" asked Lois.

"Well, me and Papa couldn't let you have a real **grizzly bear,** could we?

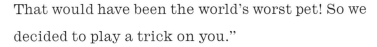

That would have been the world's worst pet! So we decided to play a trick on you."

Lois and Mylo looked at each other.

"So, Papa, you must have been Pete?" asked Lois.

"BINGO!" replied Papa.

"And all the animals?"

"Puppets operated by me!" said Daddy.

"Well, we have learned our lesson. We definitely don't want a grizzly bear as a pet, do we, Lois?" asked Mylo.

"Not in a billion bear years!" added Lois.

"Thank goodness!" replied Daddy. "I did love being Griselda, though!" he added, putting the head back on and making his best bear noise.

"GRRR!"

The four sat on the sofa and had a big family cuddle.

Then there was an unexpected sound.

TAP! TAP! TAP!

"What was that?" asked Lois.

"What was what?" said Papa.

"There was a tapping at the window!" hissed Mylo.

The family all turned round to see a real-life grizzly bear standing outside!

"GRRRR!" it growled.

It was bigger even than Griselda and was holding the jar of honey that had rolled down the hill. It had a gigantic grin on its face and was looking straight at Griselda!

"It m-m-must have c-c-come from the f-f-forest," spluttered Daddy.

"And I think it likes you, Griselda!" added Lois.

"Me?" exclaimed Daddy from under his bear outfit.

Just then the bear burst through the front door.

The family sat frozen in fear on the sofa as the bear plopped itself down next to Griselda. **PLOP!**

The bear was so heavy that the other three family members plopped off!

BOING! BOING! BOING!

The bear put its arms round Griselda and looked at her lovingly. It nuzzled its head against the fake fur.

"Oh! I love it!" said Mylo.

"Me too!" added Lois. "Let's keep it!"

The two daddies shared a look of

TERROR!

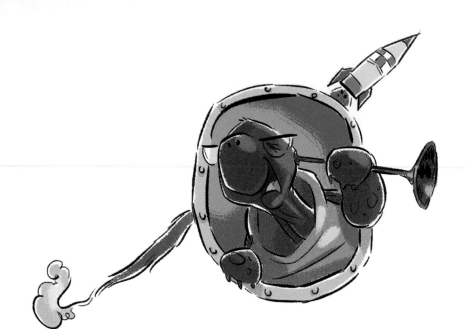

Zoom
the Supersonic
TORTOISE

IN THE BEGINNING there was an egg. From that egg came a tortoise. Deep in the mists of time, in a forgotten land, long before history began, the tortoise took its first **s l o w** steps. One day the apes leaped down from the trees, and humankind was born. The tortoise became a friend to people, a pet. The pet was passed from generation to generation to generation, until one day it found its way into the hands of a boy named Brian.

The tortoise was, in short, old.

Impossibly old.

So old that it wore spectacles, used an ear trumpet to hear and its wrinkles had wrinkles!

Brian, on the other hand, was not old – he was a child. But he was one of those children who was more like a mini grown-up. He was a shy, serious, studious little fellow. Brian's hair was neatly parted, he sported gold-rimmed spectacles and always dressed in a blazer, trousers and a tie whatever the weather. He always handed in his homework early, and carried a briefcase at all times, even on a day out to the seaside. Brian would put his candyfloss in it so he could enjoy eating it in less windy conditions.

So his father and mother (Brian and Briana) thought that a tortoise would be the perfect pet for their son.

It was quiet. Like Brian.

It walked s l o w l y, and never ran. Like Brian.

And it never came out of its shell. Like Brian.

The tortoise was bought as a twelfth birthday present for the boy.

Tortoises are widely regarded as one of the world's best pets. So how did this one end up being thought of as one of the world's worst? By doing something no tortoise had **ever** done before!

Let's return to our story to find out what that might be!

The gift of the pet was greeted with the solemnity Brian's parents had come to expect from their youngest child.

"It is a tortoise," remarked Brian after s l o w l y and methodically opening the box. Not just any tortoise but the oldest, wrinkliest tortoise you ever did see. Its half-moon spectacles were perched on its nose, and its ear trumpet held aloft.

"YIP!" went the tortoise, poking its big, pink tongue out of its tiny, wizened head as it inspected its new surroundings.

"A tortoise is a reptile, of the order of TESTUDINES, which is from the Latin word for tortoise," observed Brian.

The boy always spoke with great authority. It was as if he'd swallowed an **encyclopaedia.**

"That is correct, Brian," replied Father proudly.

"We assumed you would prefer a tortoise to a computer-game console," added Mother. She knew her son well.

"You assumed correctly, Mother," replied Brian, examining his new pet. "I have no time for computer-game consoles. For me, a tortoise is infinitely more **thrilling.**"

The tortoise smiled at this. At last, it had an owner who appreciated it!

With great care, Brian picked up the tortoise by its shell. As soon as he did, his pet retreated inside.

"SNORT!" it snorted at him.

"Oh, he seems to have gone all shy!" remarked Brian with a snort. "I, myself, am snorting because my comment is comical."

"Snort! Snort!" went his parents.

"Well, Mother, Father, thank you kindly for my birthday present."

With that, Brian patted his new pet. "If you will excuse me, I will retire to my bedroom for the evening. I have my school trip first thing in the morning to the **Science Museum** and I must rest. Goodnight!"

As the boy slowly climbed the stairs, his father said, "I have never seen Brian so excited."

"Nor me," added his mother as she watched him go.

"What a delightful chap he is!" he added.

"So unlike his sister," she replied with a grimace.

Brian tiptoed past his dreaded big sister's room. On Briana's door was a large homemade sign that read:

Once in the peace and quiet of his bedroom, Brian carefully set the tortoise down on the floor. Eventually, it appeared again out of its shell. It lumbered across the carpet so slowly

JUST GO AWAY!

you would be forgiven for thinking it wasn't moving at all. For a moment, Brian wondered whether he needed to buy his pet a walking stick to go with its spectacles and ear trumpet.

"I shall call you *ZOOM!*" announced Brian as he slid into bed. "It is another of my comical jokes!" he added, before snorting thrice. "It is funny because zooms are **very** fast, and you go incredibly s l o w l y ! I am quite the joker! **Ha! Ha!** And again **ha!**"

The tortoise shook its head. It had been around for centuries and had heard it all before.

Just then, Brian's bedroom door burst open.

BANG!

"WHAT'S THAT?" demanded the teenage girl, pointing at the tortoise, who'd once again retreated into its shell.

"It is my new pet tortoise, Zoom!"

"Tortoises are SOOO BORING!" said Briana.

"SNORT!" snorted Zoom angrily.

"No, they're not!" replied Brian.

"Yes, they are. The absolute worst! Dull! Dull! Dull!"

"Tortoises are the world's best pets!"

"Tortoises are the world's worst pets, more like!"

"How can you say that?"

"Very easily!" she replied smugly, before dancing around the room chanting: "Tortoises are the world's worst pets! Tortoises are the world's worst pets! Tortoises are the world's worst pets!"

Zoom poked its head out of its shell to see if the girl had stopped yet. When she hadn't, it retreated inside again.

"Please will you be quiet, sister?" asked Brian.

"NO!" she shouted loudly.

"You are frightening Zoom!"

"Funny name for a tortoise!"

"It was meant to be funny."

287

"Well, it's **not** funny!"

"You just said it was!"

"No, I didn't!"

Brian huffed. This was becoming tiresome. "Briana, do you have to **ruin** my birthday?"

"Oh yeah. It's your birthday. Happy stupid birthday, Loser! **Huh! Huh!**"

"So kind," replied Brian sarcastically.

Briana looked down at her brother's new pet with disgust. "That thing better not **poop** in my bedroom."

"I won't let Zoom in your bedroom, sister dearest."

"If that thing **poops** in my bedroom, I will put it between two slices of toast, add some ketchup and have a tortoise sandwich! **HA! HA!**"

Zoom was not at all happy about this. It popped out of its shell and growled. **"GRRR!"**

"Let's hope you don't choke on the shell," replied the boy sarcastically. "What a **monstrous** thing to do. As if anyone would ever eat a tortoise!" With that, Brian reached down and lifted Zoom next to him on his bed, away from his beastly sister.

"I will! If I find just one dropping from that thing in my room, it will be lunch!"

With that, Briana slammed her brother's bedroom door.

SHUNT!

Brian cuddled his tortoise, who looked more than a little frightened. "Don't be scared of her, Zoom! Perhaps I shouldn't leave you alone with my sister tomorrow. She will be at home all day revising. Or picking her nose and wiping it on my wall, more like. Would you like to come on the school trip with me?"

The tortoise nodded its head and snorted. **"SNORT!"**

"Excellent. Sweet dreams, Zoom. What do tortoises dream of? Lettuce?"

The tortoise smiled and nodded in agreement.

"I dream of lettuce too. Goodnight, Zoom."

Then he turned out the light, and the pair of new friends drifted peacefully off to sleep.

*

The **Science Museum** was Brian's dream day out, so he made sure he was up at dawn, dressed and ready for the trip, with Zoom safely in a cardboard box. It had air holes poked through so that the tortoise could breathe.

Brian took his seat at the front of the school bus with the box on his lap as the Science teacher, Miss Pry, listed all the RULES for the day.

It was like being told off before you'd had a chance to do anything wrong!

The naughty Bruiser the bully sat at the back of the bus, so it seemed only right that the nice Brian should sit at the front. Just to make sure everyone knew who the naughty one was, Bruiser very helpfully lobbed apple cores at Brian's head.

BOINK!

Every so often, Brian opened his box a tiny bit to check on his pet. He didn't want his nosy teacher to spot Zoom. Brian had read the SCHOOL RULES thoroughly. Even though tortoises were not mentioned expressly, Brian was pretty sure that, like all pets, they were forbidden at school.

"What's that in the box, Brian?" demanded Miss Pry, her eyes all googly behind her glasses.

"Nothing, miss!" he said, hurriedly shutting the box, nearly nipping Zoom's nose as he did so.

"Let me see!" she demanded.

Brian gulped. He'd never been in trouble before. With a sigh, he opened the box. The tortoise had hidden inside its shell.

"What is that?" asked Pry.

"Oh, it's my lunch, miss!" fibbed the boy. It was the first time he'd fibbed in his **entire life** and he felt a little bit **queasy!**

"You are having a tortoise shell for your lunch?" demanded an incredulous Miss Pry.

"It's not a tortoise shell," fibbed Brian, now for the second time in his life.

"Pray tell, what is it, then?"

Brian had to think fast. "A really big **croissant!**"

Pry prodded the shell with her pencil.

"It's an awfully **hard** croissant," she observed.

"It's just stale."

"If it is a croissant, as you say, then take a bite!"

Brian was **GLOWING** with **sweat.** He hated lying like this. But he was a smart kid and knew how to get out of it. "You just said that no food or drink was to be consumed on the bus. Sorry, but I would hate to break one of your **RULES,** Miss Pry."

Miss Pry harrumphed.

"HARRUMPH! I've got my eye on you, boy!"

Then the teacher returned to her seat.

Soon the bus arrived at Brian's favourite place on earth.

The **Science Museum.**

Miss Pry gathered the children outside the entrance. "Now, I want you all to eat your packed lunches before we go into the museum."

"But it's only ten o'clock in the morning, Miss Pry!" replied Brian.

"I don't want crumbs in the museum!"

"It's okay, miss. We are all kids, so we ate our packed lunches as soon as we left home," growled Bruiser, speaking for the whole group.

"Then that just leaves Brian!"

The boy gulped.

"Brian! Time to eat your giant croissant!"

Brian opened the cardboard box and took out Zoom.

"HA! HA! HA!" laughed the kids.

"That isn't a croissant!" shouted Bruiser over the noise.
"It's a turtle!"

"Tortoise, actually," snapped
Brian. "A tortoise lives on land
and a turtle lives in water."

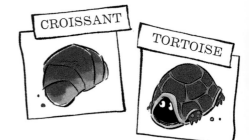

"Same difference!"

"No, it isn't!"

"I was right all along!" exclaimed a gleeful Miss Pry.
"Brian! You are in deep, deep trouble!"

"Oh no!" replied the boy. He had never been in any kind
of trouble before, let alone deep, deep trouble.

"Oh yes! The other children will enjoy a fabulous day at
the **Science Museum!**"

"Science Museum is boring, miss!" muttered Bruiser.

"And, Brian, you will have to wait outside here, facing
the wall in disgrace!"

"Can I wait outside here, facing the wall, miss?" asked
Bruiser excitedly.

"NO!"

"OOH! NOT FAIR!" moaned the bully.

"Come along, children! Let's leave this little fibber here," said Miss Pry, leading all the others inside the museum.

Brian wanted to cry. But the tortoise had an idea. It snorted to get the boy's attention. **"SNORT!"**

"What now, Zoom?" asked Brian.

The tortoise pointed round the corner to a small side window that was open.

Brian placed the tortoise under his arm, before squeezing himself through the gap in the window. Then he darted along some corridors until the pair found themselves deep inside the **Science Museum.** Brian had visited the place countless times before and so knew where all the exhibits were. He took Zoom straight to see his favourite, the space rocket.

It was a real-life one that had gone to the Moon!

"Look, Zoom! This really did *zoom* – all the way into space!"

As the boy marvelled, the tortoise was distracted by the sound of loud voices echoing across the hall. Looking around, it saw it was the school party, led by Miss Pry. Zoom snorted to alert Brian.

"SNORT!"

As soon as the boy spotted them, he hissed, "HIDE!" Yet there was nowhere to hide! They were slap bang in the middle of a wide-open space. "But where?" asked Brian.

With his front foot, the tortoise pointed to the space rocket.

"But we couldn't, could we?"

Zoom nodded as the school party approached.

Holding on tightly to the tortoise, Brian ducked under the velvet rope, before climbing into the rocket. As he clambered down into the dingy cockpit, he lost his footing and

DISASTER STRUCK!

Brian **dropped** Zoom!

CLUNK!

"SNORT!"

The tortoise had fallen through
a gap behind the seats into the engine.

"ZOOM!" called Brian.

At that moment he saw a face peering
in through the porthole.

It was Miss Pry and her prying eyes.

Just then, he felt the rocket rocking.

KERUMBLE!

When Brian popped up through the hatch, he saw that
it was Bruiser.

"Well, who's been a naughty boy, then?" growled the
bully as he rocked the rocket.

Inside, there was the sound of another **CLUNK!**

"SNORT!"

"ZOOM!" shouted Brian.

The tortoise had disappeared further down into the
engine.

KERUMBLE!

The **rocking** of the rocket caused Brian to fall too.

"ARGH!"

He fell on to a control panel, his head banging into a button.

CLICK!

All of a sudden...

WHOOMPH!

...the rocket burst into life!

"NOOOO!" cried Brian, thinking of Zoom. The tortoise was stuck in the rocket engine. It would be *frazzled!*

But then the most **amazing** thing happened!

And no one is more **amazed** than me and I am making all this stuff up!

The tortoise had **reacted** with the rocket fuel and become a...

SUPERSONIC TORTOISE!

Zoom now really could *ZOOM.*

It had turned **GOLD** and flew up through the inside of the rocket.

"SNORT!" it snorted.

Brian couldn't help but laugh at the nuttiness of it all!

"HA! HA! And again HA!"

Zoom gestured for Brian to hold on to his back. Now with the boy's hands on the tortoise's shell they rose up together through the rocket.

*✶ ═ WHOOSH! ✶

Miss Pry was so shocked that her eyes crossed, steam shot out of her ears, her face glowed as red as a raspberry and, finally, she **fainted.**

DOINK!

In mid-air, the tortoise levelled up. Brian carefully climbed on to his shell as if Zoom were a skateboard.

═ WHOOSH! ✶

"You look like a right **loon** up there!" shouted Bruiser from the ground.

"You look like a right loon **down there!**" shouted

Brian from the air.

"Come down 'ere and I'll give you a **thump!**"

"Zoom, set a course straight for Bruiser!" commanded Brian.

The tortoise smiled and did just that. He *zoomed* straight towards Bruiser.

WHOOSH!

The bully screamed, "NOOOOOOOOOOOOOOO!"

Bruiser ran through the **Science Museum** with Brian surfing on Zoom in hot pursuit.

"HHHEEELLLP!" yelled the bully.

None of the other kids did a thing to help him. They were far too busy enjoying the show. Seeing a bully finally get his just deserts was fantastic entertainment!

Bruiser sped through the museum until he reached the volcano room. In pride of place was a huge model of a volcano, as tall as a double-decker bus. It was bubbling with gallons of tomato ketchup, which represented the molten lava.

As the flying tortoise with the school swot riding it caught up with the bully, Bruiser ran up the side of the volcano to escape. When he reached the top, he turned round.

"You said you were going to give me a **thump!**" said Brian.

Bruiser grimaced and swung his fist. As he did, he lost his balance, and plunged backwards. He landed in the pool of tomato ketchup!

GLOOP!

"EURGH!" cried the boy.

"HA! HA! HA!" laughed all the other children as Bruiser, now covered from head to toe in ketchup, hauled himself out of the volcano.

The children all cheered Brian and his **SUPERSONIC TORTOISE.**

"YES!"

"WAHEY!"

"GO, BRIAN, GO!"

Brian performed a polite little bow of his head, and then asked, "Zoom, will you take us home, please?"

The tortoise snorted.

"SNORT!"

It zoomed off through the museum, much to the wonder of the visitors.

"WOW!"

"A flying tortoise!"

"Do they sell them in the gift shop?"

Then Zoom *zoomed* out of the door and high into the sky.

WHOOSH!

In no time, they had reached the family home.

"Now, let's show my big sister that tortoises are far from boring!" said Brian as they hovered outside Briana's window.

"SNORT!" — snorted Zoom in agreement.

Spying through the glass, Brian spotted his sister doing something peculiar. She was laying chocolate balls on her carpet.

"Tortoise droppings!" exclaimed the boy. "She is trying to get you into trouble!"

"SNORT!" — snorted Zoom angrily.

"Let's get her into trouble!"

So, slowly and silently, Brian lifted open her window. Then, still riding on Zoom's shell, they reversed, and zoomed as fast as they could into the girl's bedroom.

WHOOSH!

Needless to say, Briana was shocked to see her little brother skateboarding a SUPERSONIC TORTOISE.

As she stepped back, she stood on some of the hundreds of chocolate balls she had planted on her carpet. The balls *whizzed* out from under her feet, and she toppled backwards on to the floor.

THUNK!

"W-w-what's going on?" she asked, trembling.

"We could see what you were doing, trying to get Zoom into trouble!"

"It was j-j-just a j-j-joke!" she spluttered.

"Well, if you like jokes," replied Brian, "let's see if this will make you laugh!"

With that, the boy reached down to pull his sister on to the **SUPERSONIC TORTOISE'S SHELL.**

"Take us round the world, please, Zoom. As fast as you can go!"

"NOOOO!" screamed Briana.

It was too late! They were off! Zooming over or under some of the most famous buildings in the world.

When they had gone round the world at least three times...

WHOOSH!
WHOOSH!
WHOOSH!

...Briana was begging for them to "STOP!"

They *zoomed* all the way home, landing back in Briana's bedroom.

The girl slumped to the floor. "Never again, Brian! Please!"

"Do you promise to be the best sister in the world?" asked Brian.

"YES! ANYTHING!"

"Promise?"

"I PROMISE!"

"And are tortoises the world's worst pets?"

Zoom glowered at the girl.

"No," she was forced to admit. "They're the absolute best!"

"YES!" exclaimed Brian.

 **"SNORT!"** snorted Zoom.

"Right, Zoom, next stop the Moon!" ordered the boy.

Together the pair *zoomed* off into the sky, on a whole new **ADVENTURE.**

Briana looked out of the window in awe, seeing her brother and his pet light up the sky. They were heading straight for outer space.

zzZOOOOOOMMM!